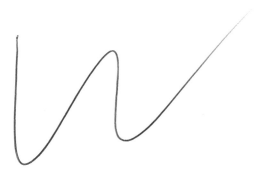

HIS QUEEN BY
DESERT DECREE

HIS QUEEN BY DESERT DECREE

LYNNE GRAHAM

MILLS & BOON

First published in Great Britain 2017
by Mills & Boon, an imprint of HarperCollins*Publishers*
1 London Bridge Street, London, SE1 9GF

Large Print edition 2018

© 2017 Lynne Graham

ISBN 978-0-263-07353-9

MIX
Paper from
responsible sources
FSC C007454

This book is produced from independently certified
FSC™ paper to ensure responsible forest management.
For more information visit www.harpercollins.co.uk/green.

Printed and bound in Great Britain
by CPI Group (UK) Ltd, Croydon, CR0 4YY

CHAPTER ONE

KING AZRAEL AL-SHARIF OF DJALIA studied the British newspaper headline with scorchingly angry dark golden eyes, his wide sensual mouth set in a harsh line. Long, luxuriant black hair fanned round his set bronzed features as he sprang upright.

'I do not think you should concern yourself with such trivia, Your Majesty,' his right-hand man, Butrus, assured him. 'What does it matter to us what other countries think? *We* know the truth. We are not backward. It is merely that Djalia's infrastructure was neglected while the dictator was in power.'

What infrastructure? Azrael almost asked, because his tiny oil-rich country was suffering from a sustained half-century of neglect. Hashem had been a cruel potentate of legendary excess, as fond of torture and killing as he had been of spending. A newly enthroned monarch, painfully aware of the trusting expectations of a people who had suffered greatly under Hashem's rule, Azrael sometimes felt weighed down by the amount of responsibility that he carried. But he was downright enraged when other countries laughed at Djalia through the offices of their media.

The newspaper showed a cart and oxen travelling down the main road of Jovan, their single city, and asked if Djalia was the most backward country in Arabia. Azrael was willing to admit that anyone looking for skyscrapers or shopping malls or fancy hotels would be disappointed because, except for a showpiece airport and an imposing motorway to the former dictator's palace, there was nothing contemporary anywhere else in the country. But given time, Djalia would move out of the Dark Ages and into the twenty-first century.

Mercifully Djalia had the wealth to power that transformation and Djalian citizens from all over the globe, medical staff, engineers and teachers, were already flooding back home to help in that Herculean task. Azrael, whose besetting sin was a serious nature that lent him a forbidding aspect beyond his thirty years of age, thought with relief about all those people coming home to help rebuild the country that he loved more than his own life. People like him who believed in religious tolerance and female equality and who desired to live in a modern, enlightened society where all had access to education and healthcare.

'You are right, Butrus. I will not concern myself with such nonsense,' Azrael acknowledged briskly. 'We must have faith in the future.'

Relieved to have lifted his monarch's mood, Butrus departed, having decided not to mention another possible problem. According to the staff at the newly opened embassy in London, Tahir, the King's younger half-brother, was infatuated with a sexy redhead. Another piece of trivia, Butrus decided loftily, for boys chased girls and that was life, although for Tahir, who had grown up in the much more restricted society of the neighbouring country of Quarein, it was undoubtedly a novelty to even be allowed to speak to an unmarried woman.

Azrael studied the walls of his twelfth-century office and then studied his desk instead. He lived and worked in a castle. He was a very fortunate man, he told himself nobly. He had refused to take up residence in the late dictator's vulgar gilded palace, which was currently being converted into an opulent and very much-needed hotel. He would not think about the reality that that palace had enjoyed an Internet connection and many other contemporary enhancements.

But he could live without those soft unnecessary extras, he assured himself. They were not necessary to a man who had spent a great deal of his life in a nomadic tent and an equal amount of it as a soldier in the desert. He was tough. He did not need such comforts. He had also known that his people did not want to see him occupying Hashem's palace, which was a symbol of both suffering and selfish extravagance. He had to show that he was different despite the blood in his veins, the blood that he fortunately also shared with his heroic father, Sharif, who had been executed for his opposition to Hashem.

A knock on the door was swiftly followed by its noisy opening, framing Butrus, who was pale as death and sporting an aghast expression. 'I am so sorry to enter in such a rude way, Your Majesty, but I'm afraid that your brother has done something *very* shocking...very shocking indeed. A huge scandal will break over our heads if we cannot find a remedy.'

A mere day before King Azrael's faith in his family's intelligence was destroyed by his brother's act of insanity, Molly remained in blissful ignorance of the storm clouds of threat gathering around her.

In fact, Molly was happy. Small and curvy, her eye-catching fall of long coppery ringlets dancing on her slim shoulders, her green eyes sparkling, she was visiting the care home where her grandfather was lodged. The home was awash with seasonal bustle and carol singers and some very tasty mince pies and the residents were thoroughly enjoying the entertainment. She gripped Maurice Devlin's gnarled hand and smiled when he mistook her for her late mother, Louise, and made no attempt to correct him. Her grandfather had dementia and his hold on faces, dates and events had slipped, allowing only brief little windows of comprehension. As he recounted a memory of some long-ago Christmas when he had chopped down a tree for his little daughter's benefit, Molly was simply delighted that he had recognised her as a relative and that he was enjoying himself.

Winterwood was a very good residential home where Maurice had received the very best of care for the past two years. Unfortunately it cost a lot of money to keep her grandfather there but Molly was very conscious that it was in the old man's best interests to keep him in familiar surroundings. A sudden change of accommodation and new faces would plunge him into severe confusion. For that reason, Molly had done everything she could to ensure that Maurice could continue to stay at Winterwood but, as she sat there holding his frail hand, she was anxiously aware that the proceeds from the sale of her mother's last piece of jewellery were almost used up. Sadly, even working night and day, she couldn't make enough cash to both live and support the top-up fees due to the care home every month.

Something would come up, she told herself optimistically, because agonising over the possibility that something might not was unproductive and Molly was a very practical young woman. As it was, Molly currently had three jobs.

During the day she worked as a waitress. At least two evenings a week she worked a cleaning shift at an office block for Jan, the friend who owned the cleaning business. And last but definitely *not* least, on weekends Molly was giving English lessons to an Arab prince at the Djalian Embassy, lessons for which she was being paid far more than all the rest of her work combined. Maybe she would suggest an extra lesson, she reasoned, but she winced at the prospect of exposing herself to spending more time with Tahir.

Although, at the same time, she reckoned she

needed to be fair to Prince Tahir because he *wasn't* harassing her. When she had told him that the flowers and the gifts he was sending her were inappropriate and unwelcome he had stopped. He had also accepted the return of the gifts and apologised profusely. He had never tried to touch her either, but his flirtatious manner and the way he studied her still unnerved her a little and it had been a relief when he'd acceded to her request that one of the embassy staff sit in on their sessions with them.

Of course, Molly would have been the first to admit that she had very little experience with men and was probably judging the young Prince too harshly. She had had to drop out of her first year on a university business course to come home and look after her grandfather and, during the subsequent four years, life as regards dating, aside of one forgettable boyfriend, had pretty much passed her by. Even so, during that period she had still contrived to pass her Teaching English as a Foreign Language qualification. Nevertheless she had no regrets about the sacrifices she had made for her grandfather because she was painfully aware that, during one of the unhappiest periods of her own life, Maurice had come to *her* rescue and had disrupted his peaceful retirement to take care of her.

Molly's mother had died when she was four and a few years later her father had remarried. His second wife had resented the very existence of her predecessor's daughter. With her father refusing to intervene to protect her from his wife's abuse, Molly's position in their household had gradually become untenable. Molly had gone to her maternal grandfather for support and he had given her a home. When her father had died, his entire estate had gone to her stepmother. That her mother's jewellery had become hers when she was still a child was only because her mother had specified that in her will.

As always at the Djalian Embassy that same afternoon, Molly marvelled at how charmingly old-fashioned it was. She gave her lessons in a formal dining room, separated from Prince Tahir by the reassuring width of a banqueting table. The door stayed open, her female chaperone seated in the hallway just outside. Directly within Molly's view hung a portrait of an eye-catching man. Mr Gorgeous, Molly had labelled him, because he had features that could have given any male supermodel a run for his money. She didn't want to think about how often Mr Gorgeous had popped up in her dreams. She supposed that what lay in her subconscious and popped up overnight was fairly similar to what many single women dreamt about if they were a little lonely and wondering when their life would finally take off and give them something more exciting to think about.

A bowing, scraping servant brought in the usual tray of coffee and Molly politely averted her eyes from the display. Clearly the young man opposite her was treated something like a deity by the embassy staff. Such effusive servility made her uncomfortable but she accepted that there were bound to be cultural differences in their lifestyles. Being a royal in Djalia was clearly a licence to inspire awe and admiration, even if Tahir was a royal from another country.

The Prince was tall enough to tower over her and she had never managed to discover exactly how old he was, stopping asking only because persistence had begun to seem impolite. However, he looked to be in his early twenties. She reckoned that some women would consider him handsome because he was built like a rugby player and had the jaw to go with it, but his lack of maturity made him unappealing to her.

'You look so beautiful today,' Tahir assured her.

'We are supposed to be making casual conversation, Your Highness,' Molly reminded him. 'Personal comments are unwise.'

He reddened, brown eyes narrowing. 'Forgive me,' he declared instantly. 'I should have said… what have you been doing today?'

'Yes, that is much better,' Molly told him with a smile and mentioned her visit to her grandfather.

'You are very lucky to have such a man in your life,' Tahir informed her. 'The only grandfather I ever knew was a monster.'

A slight frown line formed between Molly's

brows. 'That's still too personal a remark if you are with someone you don't know very well.'

'I am trying to learn you better,' Tahir responded with a hint of frustration.

'I am your teacher, not a friend,' Molly declared. 'Tell me, what have you been doing since our last session?'

'Nothing.' Tahir scrutinised the table almost guiltily as the hovering servant inched up on them to pour the coffee and settled a cup and saucer at Molly's elbow.

'I'm sure that's not true,' Molly responded, reminding herself what she was earning and knowing that she deserved it because trying to teach moody Tahir anything was like trying to push water up a hill. 'Have you gone out anywhere? You're in central London. There are so many interesting places to visit.'

'I am not a tourist. I am here only to improve my English,' Tahir responded with hauteur.

'But if you went out you would have so many more opportunities to practise your English,'

Molly replied gently, reaching for her coffee with an eager hand.

'I have no friend to go out with,' Tahir told her, regarding her with unconcealed annoyance. 'I wanted you to accompany me and then I would go many places but you said *no.*'

Molly did not want to get into the simple reality that the most senior diplomat in the embassy had advised her not to go out with Prince Tahir because it was not considered safe for him to go anywhere without bodyguards, while the presence of his bodyguards also attracted too much attention to him. Apparently, there were fears that the former overthrown Djalian dictator might have sympathisers in London, who could seek to harm a member of the royal family. That reality aside, however, Molly was grateful that she had not gone on trips with Tahir before she'd realised he was beginning to fixate on her because going any place with him would only have encouraged his interest, and it was not an interest she could reciprocate.

Molly lifted her coffee and sipped it. It was horribly sweet, which made a change from its normal bitterness. Tahir stared across the table at her, making no attempt to touch his own coffee. Surprisingly he started to talk to her then about his impressions of London. Molly realised that she felt oddly spaced out. Relieved that he was finally making an effort, though, she meant to respond to his comments but somehow her brain was too fuzzy for concentration.

Her head felt heavy on her neck and she registered that she felt ridiculously sleepy. She propped her chin on her upturned hand. 'I think I must be very tired,' she framed, noticing that her voice emerged sounding slurred. 'Something is wrong with me...'

'Nothing is wrong,' Tahir told her soothingly.

With an enormous effort of will, Molly planted her hands down on the surface of the table and pushed upright. Her cup and saucer slid off the edge of the table and tumbled with a crash on the tiled floor and she studied the broken pieces with a detached interest that felt as strange to her as her heavy, paralysed body.

'I'm ill…need help,' she mumbled on a very sudden flash of fear.

'I will help you,' Tahir assured her, moving towards her. 'You will be fine. I promise you.'

'Don't want your help,' Molly slurred, stubborn to the last, but her tongue felt too thick for her mouth and the effort it required to even focus her gaze was too much for her. Her eyes slid shut and she slumped down over the table.

Molly woke, feeling wonderfully comfortable. Slowly lifting her head, she opened her eyes and stared in shock at her completely unfamiliar surroundings.

She was lying on a bed in a room with bare stone walls that looked positively medieval. She sat up, discovering that she was wearing a white floaty cotton garment that did not belong to her, and she leapt off the ornate bed in growing consternation to rush over to the window. The landscape beyond that window made her brain short-circuit for several terrifying seconds. There was a desert outside, an actual *desert* with towering sand dunes that reminded her of a picture she had once seen of the Sahara. Her mouth ran dry.

How the heck had she travelled from the Djalian Embassy in London to…? And then she remembered the sweet coffee, her strange symptoms and then what must have been her collapse. She had been drugged. Was that too melodramatic an assumption? Molly was a very down-to-earth young woman and the concept of being drugged and kidnapped initially struck her as too fantastic an explanation to be possible. But then there was the unusually sweet coffee, she recalled, along with Prince Tahir watching her and telling her that she would be fine even though she had patently not been fine. Molly breathed in deep and slow.

'Mees Carlisle?' a soft female voice enquired, making her jump and spin in dismay. A young woman, clad in a long dress, was anxiously peering at her through a doorway. 'I am Gamila and I am to tell you that you are safe. *Safe*,' she repeated the word with emphasis. 'No English,' she completed apologetically.

'Safe?' Molly whispered shakily, suddenly realising that what had happened to her was real and not the result of a waking dream or her imagination. 'Where am I?'

But the young woman was busy spreading open the door to display a bathroom and Molly was too grateful to see one to persist in enquiries that her companion seemed unable to answer. She closed the door, discovering a new toothbrush awaited her as well as soap and other necessities. *Had* Tahir kidnapped her? And if so, where was he now? Dear heaven, was he a madman? A sex offender? Had she been teaching English to a seriously dangerous man all these weeks?

Filled with horror and conjecture on worst-case scenarios, Molly ran herself a shallow bath, there being no shower, which surprised her because the bathroom suite and the tiling looked brand new. She was safe, she reminded herself doggedly. Someone had taken the time and trouble to coach Gamila into repeating that message…she was *safe*. But telling herself that even as she towelled herself dry did not make her feel remotely safe in such a strange environment.

She was abroad *without* a passport, she thought fearfully. She didn't own a passport because she had never travelled abroad. Her father had not been a fan of foreign holidays and she had never had enough money to plan such a trip for herself. But when she had studied for her TEFL qualification, it had been her dream to work and live abroad. *The only grandfather I ever knew was a monster*, Tahir had said. Maybe she should have listened harder because it seemed to her that Tahir took after him. Only a monster with a nasty agenda would drug and carry off a woman to a foreign country. Where were the police? Molly wanted to see a policeman and report her abduction...*then* she would feel safe from all threat.

A long dress like Gamila's hung on a hook on the wall. Since her own clothing was nowhere to be seen and Molly felt too exposed in the thin nightie she wore, she put on the dress after ascertaining that it at least smelled as if it was new. Even so, she had no underwear and Molly winced at the lack of a bra because she was extra curvy in the breast department. She had always hated that about her body, she reflected ruefully. Overly generous curves at breast and hip had bloomed as soon as she reached puberty. All very well had such curves been grafted onto a taller body, she conceded, but not so welcome a gift for a girl who barely passed five feet in height.

She emerged from the bathroom to find Gamila waiting for her with a tray of food. Molly studied the tray with distrust. Tahir had drugged her. How did she know the food was harmless? She shook her head in refusal although she was very hungry, and went back into the bathroom to use the tumbler by the sink to drink some tap water, simply praying that the source was hygienic. Gamila, looking puzzled by that demonstration, set the tray down and left the room.

Molly stood at the window staring out at that unbelievable view of the sand dunes. The sun was lower in the sky, turning them a toasty gold shade which was unexpectedly beautiful. It was time for her to find out where she was and when she was getting home, *after* she had reported Tahir to the authorities. As she stalked to the door in a fine temper a knock sounded on it. She flung it wide.

'I...' and then her tongue simply glued to the roof of her mouth because it was Mr Gorgeous from the portrait in the embassy hallway.

There he stood, in his pristine white robes and red chequered head cloth, those stunning features even more arresting in the flesh. It was as if a famous actor had stepped out of a movie screen into her presence. She was deeply shaken and she could barely breathe for nerves. In discomfiture, she backed away fast until her legs hit the very solid wooden bed frame behind her.

'Miss Carlisle? I am Azrael, Tahir's half-brother,' Azrael proffered, rigid in bearing and stilted in speech from the sheer shame of what his little brother had done. 'I must offer you my most profound apologies for what has happened to you and I assure you that you will be taken home as soon as possible.'

A tiny bit mollified by that unexpectedly humble approach from a man who looked more as if he should be waving a scimitar from the back of a horse in battle, so fierce was his expression, Molly moved forward a step. He was incredibly tall, well over six feet in height. And those eyes, a part of Molly that embarrassed her noted without her volition, he had the most *amazing* dark golden eyes, so heavily lashed in black that he looked as though he were sporting eye liner.

'You speak English,' she heard herself say rather stupidly.

'I do,' Azrael acknowledged, studying her with a concealed appreciation that affronted him, for he did not want to believe that he had the smallest taste in common with a brother who had committed such a very unforgivable act against a woman. But Tahir had more taste than his elder brother would have given him credit for. For some reason, Azrael had been expecting to see a Westernised blonde of pretty obvious attractions.

Instead he had Molly Carlisle before him and there was no contest in that comparison. Her skin was as fine and fair as pearlised silk. She had an astonishing colour of hair such as Azrael had never seen before and a wonderful wealth of it, and eyes the exact shade of his late mother's famous emeralds. She was a beauty, a truly unusual beauty. His thoughts, his very awareness, were inappropriate, *deeply* inappropriate in the circumstances, Azrael castigated himself angrily, suppressing his too personal reactions to the very best of his ability.

'When are the police coming?' Molly asked baldly.

Nothing could have more surely focused Azrael's concentration back on his dilemma than that innocent question. In point of fact, Djalia did not currently have a police force, Hashem's police department having been wholly corrupt. A large new group of male and female applicants was currently in training but, of course, he was not going to tell *her* that there were no police and expose his much-maligned country to adverse criticism again.

'It is my hope that we can settle this unfortunate matter without alerting the authorities,' Azrael told her truthfully, resting the full force of his commanding eyes on her, his royal resolve driving him. He knew how authoritative he was and how intimidating he could be and he was prepared to use that strength against her if necessary. Regardless of the cost, he *had* to protect Djalia from an international scandal and the risk of the rest of the world finding out what had happened and assuming that they were all ignorant, woman-stealing savages.

Impervious to his extremely bossy manner and commanding stance, because she was immovable when she made her mind up about anything, Molly compressed her lips. 'I'm afraid not. I want the police. I want your brother…half-brother, whatever he is, prosecuted and punished.'

Taken aback by her complete lack of reaction to his royal poise, Azrael expelled his breath in a measured hiss. 'There will be no police involved,' he informed her flatly.

'I've been drugged and kidnapped. I *demand* justice!' Molly launched at him full throttle.

'I must apologise for my inability to meet your demand. My brother is no longer in Djalia to be prosecuted,' Azrael countered, deciding to pursue another tack.

'I don't believe you,' Molly responded, shocking him with that frank admission, for he had never had the veracity of his words questioned before by anyone. 'You're trying to protect him from the consequences of what he's done—'

'That is not the case,' Azrael assured her, and it was the truth because at that moment he would happily have thrown Tahir to the wolves had that been an option but, sadly, it was not.

'You cannot deny me my rights,' Molly began, rosy colour mantling her cheeks as fury began to suffuse her, firing through her veins like an intoxicating drug.

His eyes hard as granite, Azrael's jaw clenched. 'I *can*—'

'You *can't*!' Molly spat back at him in a rage. 'You can't deny me my rights. There are international laws protecting women—'

'Not in Djalia,' Azrael told her truthfully but without pride.

'I was drugged and kidnapped—'

'But Tahir was intercepted as soon as the plane landed and you were immediately removed from his keeping. You are unharmed,' Azrael reminded her.

'But I *could've* been the victim of sexual violence!' Molly shot at him with knotted fists, her temper only rising at his refusal to do a single thing that she asked.

'I doubt that. Tahir is many foolish things but he's not a rapist. He thought he could bring you here and shower you with clothes and jewels and that then you would magically find him more appealing,' Azrael recited with derision. 'He is infatuated with you but he would never have physically harmed you.'

'So, in your opinion, it's basically all right for him to have drugged and kidnapped me?'

'No, of course it is not right, it is very *wrong*!' Azrael proclaimed heatedly, his own temper flaring at her wording. 'It was a crime and there is no dispute on that issue but we will not involve the police in this matter.'

'That's not your decision to make,' Molly told

him angrily, green eyes glittering like jewels, coppery ringlets dancing across her slim shoulders with the livewire energy of her every restive movement.

'It *is* my decision,' Azrael contradicted softly, wondering what colour would best describe that dark red and yet strangely bright hair and furiously repressing the irrelevant thought. 'And in Djalia *my* word is law.'

'Then Djalia must be a pretty backward place!' Molly hurled back at him loudly.

Azrael froze as if she had thrown a flaming torch at him, every line of his lean, extravagantly handsome face drawn taut with offence and growing anger. 'I will not discuss this business again with you until you have calmed down and thought it over.'

'I'm as calm as I'm ever going to be after waking up to see a desert out of the freakin' window!' Molly flung hotly and as he turned on his heel, making her realise that he intended to leave again, she was fit to be tied. 'Don't you dare walk out of here and leave me!'

'You are not in a mood to be reasonable—'

'How blasted reasonable would you be after being drugged and kidnapped?' Molly shouted after him, and she kicked the door shut with a resounding clunk on his sweeping departure. She hurt her bare toes and cursed and hopped round the room, ineffectually trying to soothe them while boiling with frustrated fury at Tahir's brother.

Clearly insanity ran in the family! One abducted her to a foreign country and the other wanted her to be *reasonable*. What century was he living in? What kind of country was Djalia where women had no rights and some good-looking louse could tell her and with a straight face, mind you, that *his* word was law? Who the blazes did he think he was to talk to her like that? Well, Molly had no intention of standing for that kind of nonsense. His countrywomen might have no rights, but she knew she had hers and she had every intention of exercising them in the UK, if need be, where the crime had taken place. Yes, she registered belatedly, Azrael's attitude didn't really matter because she could go to the police at home and report the crime once she got back there. And he couldn't stop her doing that, could he?

As if she cared about Tahir or what happened to him! She wanted to know that Tahir would be punished and that he could never, ever do to any other woman what he had done to her. As for that assurance that Tahir would never have physically harmed her, Molly was not impressed. Did she look stupid enough to credit that Tahir had gone to such extraordinary lengths merely to offer her new clothes and jewels? No, she would ensure that the British police dealt with Tahir.

Mollified by that idea, Molly greeted the surprised Gamila with a smile when she crept in carrying Molly's freshly laundered clothes. Thanking the other woman, Molly vanished into the bathroom to put on her own clothes, snapping her bra on again with deep satisfaction and shimmying into her jeans and sweater. Only as perspiration began to gather on her skin and her face did she appreciate that what she had worn for a London winter was quite unsuitable for a desert climate. Crossly she stripped again and put the stupid dress back on because at least it was cool and comfortable.

Leaving the bedroom, she walked out onto a stone corridor and espied a worn spiral staircase, brows climbing at the sight of it. She walked down into a square turreted forecourt of some kind that was crowded with uniformed soldiers carrying guns, all of whom turned to stare at her in the most unsettling way. Taken aback, she coloured and froze and was grateful when a wiry little man in robes hailed her from several feet away. 'Miss Carlisle? How may I assist you?'

'I want to speak to Azrael again,' Molly said, moving towards him. 'I want to go home.'

'Of course. Please come this way. I am Butrus. I work for the King.'

'What king?' Molly almost whispered.

'His Majesty, King Azrael of Djalia,' Butrus proclaimed with clear pride. 'Our Glorious Leader.'

Glorious Leader? Oh, how Molly enjoyed that label and she would have struggled not to laugh at it in any other mood but her aggression had been swallowed alive by mind-blowing surprise. Tahir's brother was the *King* of this country? That was why there had been that portrait hung in the Djalian Embassy, she realised belatedly. But Tahir had not mentioned his big brother's exalted status, possibly because he lived in a different country. Molly had looked up Quarein on the Internet, not Djalia, and she knew nothing whatsoever about the country she had landed in.

'I didn't realise he was the King,' Molly admitted thinly, not best pleased to accept her own ignorance.

But it didn't essentially change anything, she reasoned angrily. She now understood why Azrael could declare that his word was law in Djalia and not be carted away to the funny farm. She also understood that he had much more power over the situation than she had initially appreciated. Well, that was good, Molly thought grimly. With his influence, he would surely be able to get her home to London even faster. And she had to get back, *had* to get home to be available for Maurice should he need her. After all, she was her grandfather's only relative and his only representative and she needed to be on the spot to ensure that his needs were always met and that he received the best possible care.

CHAPTER TWO

AZRAEL'S HEART SANK when Butrus ushered Molly Carlisle into the library of his desert fortress, where he normally contrived to relax. In truth, while deeply resenting the position he found himself in when he had done nothing wrong, he had had enough of her for one day. But he straightened his broad shoulders, reminded himself of his duty to Djalia and felt ashamed of that momentary shrinking from what had become necessity.

Whether he liked it or not, he *had* to placate Molly Carlisle. It didn't matter how much money it cost to buy her silence. It didn't matter even that bribery of any kind appalled him and contravened his values. Butrus was correct: 'needs must when the devil rides', some homely but apt saying the older man had picked up from his Scottish grandmother. But the entire distasteful business might have been more bearable had he found Tahir's victim less attractive, he conceded grudgingly.

Of course, he couldn't remember when he had last had sex. That was probably all that was amiss with him: the weight of a celibate life. Not that, strictly speaking, he was *expected* to be celibate but he could only relax and enjoy his sensual nature outside Djalian borders because to do otherwise could risk attracting unsavoury comparisons with Hashem's orgies with his so-called concubines. Unhappily for Azrael, the time and freedom to travel abroad where casual affairs were not seized on and dissected did not feature in his current crammed schedule. And he had already learned that nothing he did, nowhere he went and nobody he even spoke to was considered too trivial to provide fodder for the Djalian free press. His every word, his every act was reported on. Only here in the desert at the fortress built by his ancestors was he usually left alone in peace.

And absolutely the very last thing he needed in his sensitised radius was a woman with a shape that even in a long dress was impossible to ignore. She had hourglass curves, an incredibly womanly figure and a luscious full mouth that would put X-rated images into the head of a saint. And he was no saint. At heart he was merely a man like any other with all a normal man's needs and wants and he really did not wish to be reminded of that exasperating reality when he could do nothing to assuage his libido.

Mr Gorgeous looked more like Mr Grumpy, Molly reflected, noting the hard lines etched into his stunning features. Sadly, it didn't detract in the slightest from his male beauty, although she was irritated that his head was covered and she couldn't see his hair to see if it was as dark as his brother's. She *liked* looking at him, no harm in that, she rationalised. It wasn't as though she liked anything he said or anything he did and finding out that he was a *king* was downright off-putting because how was someone as ordinary as she was supposed to know how to tiptoe politely round his royal sensibilities? She didn't like him; he didn't like her. She could see his animosity in the steely glint in his darker-than-dark eyes, the flare of his classic nose, the challenging angle of his jaw and the set compression of his full male lips.

His hostility wasn't a problem for her though, she thought ruefully. All she wanted was to go home, back to the life she had been very rudely ripped from, and no haughty, proud royal personage would deflect her from her rights or her wishes.

'I'm not easily impressed, Your Majesty, but I do apologise if anything I said earlier caused offence.' Molly trotted out her prepared opening speech, seeing the point of smoothing her way in advance with a little civility. It was surface-thin civility but he didn't know that, did he?'

Azrael's lip curled because he could read insincerity at twenty paces and her eyes told him the truth that her voice did not. Even so, he was equally willing to dissemble if it solved the problem. 'It is forgotten,' he assured her. 'How may I help you?'

'I want to go home...as quickly as that can be arranged,' Molly admitted.

'And your desire to see my brother prosecuted?' An ebony brow lifted enquiringly.

Involuntarily, Molly flushed. 'Is unchanged but I've realised that the crime would be more properly handled where it occurred...in London.'

'Naturally I do not want that.'

Molly tossed back her head, rich coppery ringlets rippling back from her cheeks. 'I fail to see why,' she admitted bluntly. 'You weren't involved in what your brother did, were you?'

'No, but the crime took place in my country's embassy and at my brother's request a member of embassy staff illegally acquired the drug used to sedate you. Tahir then brought you here to Djalia, intending to transport you to this fortress, which belongs to me. The reputation of Djalia and my own reputation is thus very much *involved* in this offensive matter,' Azrael told her with equal directness. 'The member of staff has been returned here to face charges of drug abuse and the servant who assisted my brother in his wrongdoing has been dismissed.'

'How was I transported here?' Molly queried uneasily.

'The women in Tahir's birth country, Quarein, wear full veils. You were veiled and conveyed through the airport in a wheelchair and no questions were asked because my brother holds diplomatic status. You were put in the cabin of the private jet owned by Tahir's father, Prince Firuz, the ruler of Quarein, and were still there when the jet was boarded at our airport. The steward was so concerned by your unconscious condition that he instructed the female stewardess to remain with you throughout the flight. He also alerted Tahir's father, who immediately contacted me. At no stage were you left open to any form of abuse.'

Molly swallowed hard on her relief because in the back of her mind she had worried about what could have happened to her body while she was unconscious and had scolded herself for her fears. She breathed in slowly. 'That is good,' she muttered a little unevenly as she looked down at the worn mosaic tiled floor, embarrassed by her secret apprehension that she could have been touched while she was unaware of it.

For a split second, she looked so vulnerable that Azrael's conscience propelled him forward one dangerous step to offer inappropriate sympathy before he stopped himself in his tracks. 'I do recognise that you have suffered a very traumatic experience,' he breathed almost harshly. 'And I deeply regret that a member of my family subjected you to such an ordeal, but be assured that Tahir will be most severely punished. His father is horrified by what he has done—'

'That means nothing to me,' Molly broke in quickly, keen to forestall such a shift in their dialogue because Tahir's family was not her concern.

'Quarein is much stricter than Djalia when it comes to relations between men and women,' Azrael extended, royally ignoring her interruption. 'In Quarein the sexes are segregated and women are very much protected. Men are executed for crimes against women there.'

'And not *here*?' Molly could not resist asking.

'While Hashem was in power here, men were executed daily for every kind of crime, many for very small crimes and many who were innocent of *any* crime other than opposition to his regime,' Azrael told her with gravity. 'It was an inhumane system.'

'It's not my business anyway,' Molly backtracked hurriedly, wondering how she had got led into such a discussion. 'My only interest here is in how soon I can go home.'

Azrael opted for honesty. 'I do not want to release you only for you to return to London to pursue Tahir's prosecution. I will do almost anything to avoid that happening because I will not have Djalia damaged in the fallout from such an appalling scandal.'

It was his wording that unnerved Molly. Talk of 'releasing' her implied that she was not free to leave when she wished. 'Am I a prisoner here, then?'

Azrael sidestepped that leading question. 'I am determined to settle this affair for once and all with you *before* you go home.'

A pair of green eyes inspected him with a level of scorn Azrael had never met in a woman's gaze before. 'And how do you plan to *settle* it?'

Ironically, Azrael was grateful to be urged to that distasteful point. 'By compensating you liberally for your ordeal in return for your silence.'

Molly was very much taken aback by that declaration. 'You're offering me money to keep quiet?' she gasped in disbelief.

'Compensation,' Azrael framed, wishing he could gag her to force her to listen, wishing she weren't acting shocked because he had been shocked by the concept too until Butrus had laid out all the possibilities before him. He did not wish to see any admirable qualities in her because it only intensified the attraction of something that could never ever be.

After all, in all likelihood he would be married in a few months. He would probably accept the bride from Quarein his stepfather had already suggested to him. Nasira was Prince Firuz's niece and Azrael had met her when they were both still children, thinking even then that she was rigorously well behaved and very devout. Why did those worthy assets turn him off rather than turn him on? He didn't want to think about that. He had yet to meet Nasira as an adult and if Prince Firuz's wishes were followed, he would not get the chance to meet her before marrying her because that was the tradition in Quarein. Worryingly however, a veiled queen would be a retrograde choice in the eyes of his people, whose women had never worn the veil.

'But money,' Molly responded in unconcealed disgust. 'I want justice, *not* money!'

'Perhaps in an ideal world,' Azrael countered. 'Unfortunately, it is not an ideal world that we live in.'

'My desire to have your brother prosecuted is stronger than my desire for money,' Molly assured him fiercely. 'I am not a forgiving woman.'

'With respect, I suggest that you consider my offer,' Azrael advised with icy cool, the hauteur of his finely sculpted features intense. 'If you do not consider it, we are at stalemate and, as you have already said, you *want* to go home.'

Something inside Molly just snapped wide open and let out a flood of pent-up anger. Mr Gorgeous was a complete seven-letter word and she was tempted to land him a punch for his nerve in saying that to her. She had been drugged and kidnapped and now pressure was being put on her to accept financial compensation in place of a prosecution! How *dared* he? How dared he assume that she was the sort of woman who could be bought off? It was true that she was poor and had to work for a living and that more money would certainly come in very handy, particularly with regard to the cost of Maurice's care, she acknowledged reluctantly, but she also had principles and she knew right from wrong.

'A crime has to have a punishment,' she shot back at him, her raised voice reverberating at an embarrassing volume up through the domed ceiling above them. '*Nothing* else is acceptable to me!'

'If that is the case I am sorry for it,' Azrael grated, thoroughly tired of the way she shouted at him. She was a hot-tempered virago of a woman, he decided, pleased to have found a fatal flaw hidden at the very heart of such beauty. As a man who rarely lost his own temper, he had little tolerance for those with less control. Furthermore, he hadn't been shouted at since he was a soldier in training and it was one aspect of military life that he did not miss.

'And I am sorry that you are a king who does not appear to know right from wrong,' Molly fired back with an unconcealed contempt that sent Azrael's stunning deep-set eyes flaring to a scorching rage-filled gold.

But, raised in a much harsher school than she had been, Azrael gritted his teeth and exerted restraint over the teeming volatile emotions he had learned to rise above as a teenager when, innocent of fault, he had been whipped and humiliated. He had taken his punishment like a man to protect his mother. He knew that he could withstand any punishment to protect his country. And what were words? Opinions? Was he so weak that he could even react to such a condemnation from someone who knew nothing of the sacrifices he had been forced to make throughout his life? No, he was not weak.

In a stormy tempest of fury, Molly raced back up the spiral staircase and felt momentarily dizzy, realising then that it was a very long time since she had last eaten. Gamila appeared with another tray while Molly was struggling to decide what to do next. This time, Molly accepted the meal, acknowledging that Azrael was unlikely to be planning to either drug or poison her. Was she being naïve though? Should she be scared? Azrael was determined to prevent her from returning home to report Tahir's crime and clearly hoping that time would take care of her opposition.

Well, she had already lost her waitressing job. A failure to turn up for her shift was all that would take, she reflected gloomily. Was she being naïve about her safety in this desert castle? Wouldn't it suit everyone here very well if she were simply to disappear? A cold shiver snaked down her spine despite the humidity. Nobody back home even knew where she was, nor would anyone find out. Her friend, Jan, would try to phone her and then might mistakenly assume that she had found more lucrative part-time work. Sadly, Molly worked such long hours that she had had little recent time free to catch up with Jan, who had recently given birth to her first child.

She shouldn't have eaten that food, she thought fearfully. How could she possibly be *safe* in Djalia when so much appeared to hinge on her keeping quiet about Tahir's crime? And here she was refusing and arguing with the Djalian King, who froze into an ice statue of chilly dignity every time she raised her voice. Not exactly the way to make friends and have a positive influence on people, was it?

But she was a victim and she wanted the perpetrator punished. Was that *so* wrong? Unnerved by her own flailing thoughts, Molly sat there wondering what to do next. She refused to be coerced into not doing what she had the right to do and that was reporting Tahir to the UK police. No doubt there would be some people back home just as eager to make the story go away if offending people in high places in an oil-producing country would result. No, she was not that naïve, but she was also determined.

And if Azrael wasn't prepared to return her to the airport she would get herself there. It couldn't be far away. Djalia was a tiny country, wasn't it? She seemed to recall Tahir making some remark of that nature, a vaguely derogatory one. And if she had been recovered *at* the airport and brought to the fortress it was unlikely that the airport could be that far away, she reasoned, immediately feeling more upbeat about her prospects of escape under her own steam. Why should she sit here acting like a willing prisoner?

She was utterly innocent of fault in what had happened. But *did* Azrael believe that? Or did he suspect that she had encouraged Tahir in his delusions? She knew that there were women who would have encouraged Tahir simply because he was rich and willing to buy expensive gifts but she wasn't one of them. But did Azrael know that or did he believe the worst of her? Sixth sense suggested that Azrael cherished a half-empty-cup view of life while she preferred the half-full-cup version. He would believe the worst and, in the circumstances, be glad to believe the worst of her if it made his half-brother's wrongdoing seem more understandable and more forgivable.

It would undoubtedly not occur to Azrael that she was a good deal less experienced with men than most women in her age group. Had that not been the case, would there have been anything in Tahir's attitude that she would have recognised as threatening? Could she somehow have averted that threat? How could she tell? Aside of the few casual dates she had enjoyed as a schoolgirl and the single boyfriend she had had since her grand-father went into care, Molly had had neither the freedom nor the time to explore the world of sex. The boyfriend had been short-lived because she hadn't particularly enjoyed his kisses and when he had demanded more she had ditched him, reck-oning that if he had been right for her she would have wanted to have sex with him, instead of being repulsed by the idea of it. There was the possibility, though, she conceded wryly, that she had a naturally low sex drive because she was not remotely bothered by her lack of experience and only very mildly curious about what she might be missing. Although, if she was honest, she reflected grudgingly, she had been considerably more curious since she first laid eyes on Azrael...

But what on earth did it matter what Azrael thought of her? Why would she even care?

Well, the unwilling prisoner was about to make a run for it, Molly decided. Recalling all those soldiers on the floor below, she realised she would have to wait until night fell and most people were asleep and then creep out. Buoyed up by the belief that she could thumb her nose at Azrael's coercion and escape Djalia, Molly lay back on her bed, smiling for the first time that day. Throwing a spanner in the works of Azrael's god complex held immense appeal for her.

Luckily she hadn't unsealed the water bottle that had arrived with her very tasty meal. She wasn't stupid enough to think that she could head into the desert heat without water, but she wondered how far and in which direction the nearest road lay. Positioning herself by the window for a couple of hours, she kept watch for vehicles, and there were several four-wheel-drive rough-terrain cars that rolled down the dunes but they all traversed the same route, she noted with satisfaction. She would follow their tracks out back to civilisation and freedom.

'Tahir will be harshly punished by his father,' Butrus reminded his monarch. 'Prince Firuz is a severe man.'

'As I have cause to know,' Azrael reminded the older man wryly, for Firuz was his stepfather.

Some years after Azrael's father had been executed in Djalia, Azrael's mother had returned to Quarein and remarried. The following year Tahir had been born. A former princess of Quarein, Azrael's mother's marriage to the ruling sheikh of Quarein had been as much a political alliance to strengthen her teenaged son's standing as a personal relationship. Always guiltily aware of that truth, Azrael had grimly tolerated Firuz's tough parenting regime and pitied his kid brother for what lay ahead of him.

'He will not escape a whipping,' Butrus mused out loud with a faint but perceptible shudder. 'You should tell Miss Carlisle that. Tahir will pay heavily for his stupidity. His father will ensure it. Prince Firuz makes no allowance for youthful mistakes.'

'Unhappily for Tahir, this was much worse than youthful idiocy. It was a crime,' Azrael pronounced stonily. 'I feel dirtied by the whole business. For the first time in my life I have threatened a woman.'

'Our country comes first and last,' his advisor murmured heavily. 'Occasionally there will be a need to face repugnant choices and choose the lesser of two evils.'

Azrael excused himself for the night. His brain recognised that Butrus was correct and that being a king would sometimes plunge him into contentious issues, but in his heart he was too conflicted to accept it. He had always tried to be an honourable, decent man but now he was utilising coercion on an innocent woman and the necessity of that treatment inflamed his pride and his own sense of justice. *He* felt guilty now.

About an hour before dawn, Molly crept down the spiral staircase carrying her shoes, the little tube of lip salve she had had in the pocket of her jeans and the bottle of water in a carrier bag she had found stuffed in the bathroom cabinet. She had tucked in a towel to cover her head from the heat because she had no hat to use. She had left her jeans behind, seeing no reason to burden herself with having to carry anything she couldn't use. The forecourt, which had been so busy earlier in the day, was deserted but for one soldier stationed by the wall smoking. She lurked in the shadows until he began patrolling the battlements again and turned his back to the steps that led down to the next level. Then quick as a flash she darted out into view barefoot and sped down the steps.

There appeared to be no more guards but she still had to find her way out of the fortress. Fortunately for her, everywhere seemed to be deserted and she went down another flight of steps to find herself in a walled courtyard with closed gates and a pack of parked four-wheel drives. She wished she could steal a car and wondered what the punishment for that would be in Djalia. But starting up a car engine would attract attention, wouldn't it? *Or would it?* Vehicles had been coming and going at all hours late into the night while she'd watched. At the same time she doubted her ability to drive up a steep sand dune and feared coming to grief at that first hurdle.

Picking her way between the cars while on the watch for anyone moving, she reached the gates and, with all the strength she had, she thrust down the iron bar on the gate to open it. As it creaked noisily open she slid out through the gap with a fast-beating heart and fled.

CHAPTER THREE

MOLLY RAN UP the dune through the deep pitted tracks left by the cars, desperate not to be spotted by guards at the fortress before she could get out of sight. She reached the peak and, because it was much colder than she had expected, she drew in a deep breath and kept on running, grateful that she was fit. Running was, after all, what she did for exercise at home, but running in a dress was another story altogether, she discovered, with the stretch of her legs restricted and her strides shortened. She thought about simply pulling the dress up to her waist but, although she could see no sign of life in the moonlit landscape, she didn't want to expose herself in her underwear in a country where that was probably unacceptable.

She stayed on the tracks but they mysteriously petered out around the time the sun started rising and the glare of that alone made studying her surroundings a challenge. She was looking for a landmark of some kind to take as a direction to ensure that she didn't get lost, but all she could see was marching lines of sand dunes. *What did you expect?* she asked herself irritably. *A signpost to the airport?*

Well, no, but she had hoped to find a recognisable road at least, only there wasn't a road or tracks anywhere that she could see. Yet the cars must have travelled from somewhere, she thought in frustration, veering off to the left when she espied flatter land there because climbing a dune without tracks was too difficult and too tiring to get her anywhere fast. A stony plain stretched before her then, occasional small bits of vegetation appearing, which persuaded her that she was heading in the right direction and likely to draw closer to what she dimly thought of as civilisation. Buildings, roads, cars...*people*. It infuriated her that probably all those things were close by, but she couldn't spot them because of the blasted dunes blocking her view. She stilled a few times and simply listened, hoping to catch sounds that would lead her in a certain direction, but there was nothing, only the soft noise of the light breeze in her eardrums and the fast beat of her own heart. While she was sipping her water, mindful that she needed to conserve it, however, Azrael was shouting for the first time in all the years Butrus had known him.

'How could any woman be that stupid?' he was demanding wrathfully soon after Gamila had discovered her unoccupied bed and a search had established that Azrael's guest was no longer anywhere on the premises. 'There is nothing out there but miles and *miles* of desert.'

'But Miss Carlisle doesn't know that…unless someone mentioned it,' Butrus remarked, looking at no one in particular. 'She will soon get tired and too hot and come back. Perhaps she simply went for a walk—'

'A…*a walk*?' Azrael erupted afresh in disbelief. 'She has run away! She is a very stubborn, determined woman. I tell you…she has run away *because* I told her that she couldn't leave!'

'It is a source of greater concern to me that any-one was able to leave without a single guard chal-lenging them,' admitted Halim, the commanding officer of Azrael's household guard, with a frown. 'There will be an investigation into that worry-ing event after the woman is found. If someone can get out so easily, someone *could* have got in and reached His Majesty—'

'His Majesty is very well able to defend him-self!' Azrael bit out rawly. 'I am going out to look for her—'

'I would not advise that,' Butrus interposed, forgetting his usually punctilious manners in his dismay.

'Nobody knows this part of the desert better than me...nobody is a better tracker!' Azrael fired back at him with unarguable assurance.

'But a severe sandstorm is due to move in be-fore nightfall,' Halim reminded his royal em-ployer nervously. 'You must not put yourself at risk when there is no need. The whole guard are already out there searching for her.'

But Azrael had always been stubborn as a rock

and highly resistant to advice. He felt personally responsible for Molly's disappearance and if anything happened to her he knew he would carry the shame of it to the end of his days. Furthermore, having spent his childhood at the fortress and many months in almost the same locality as an adolescent following his father's execution, he did know the terrain better than anyone else available. When he had changed into more suitable desert apparel, the dark blue robes of his nomadic heritage, he politely refused Halim's companionship, knowing that Halim's disability would make hours on horseback a day of physical suffering for him. Halim had stumbled on a landmine during the struggle to topple Hashem from power.

'You are not to take such risks.' Butrus was still protesting Azrael's involvement right to the door of the stables. 'If anything happens to you, what happens to Djalia? You agreed with the council… *no more personal risks.*'

'Don't be silly, Butrus. This is an emergency,' Azrael responded squarely. 'I will scarcely come to harm in a storm. I was a member of our special forces. There is nothing the desert can throw at me that I cannot handle.'

'The woman is not worth the danger to your life,' Butrus breathed, his voice quavering with emotion.

Azrael was taken aback to see the level of concern in his adviser's eyes and he gave his shoulder a rather awkward pat before vaulting up onto the back of his horse. 'No one life is worth more than another. You taught me that,' he reminded him with quiet authority.

'I spoke in error.' Butrus was still arguing vigorously as Azrael rode out of the courtyard.

Around the same time, Molly was beginning to realise that she might have made a very bad decision when she left the fortress. Once she crossed the flat plain to reach the one and only landmark she had even seen since venturing out, she knew she was weakening. The heat was unbelievable. She had never felt heat of that magnitude in her life. The sun above was relentless and the sand was scorching, burning her feet even through the soles of her canvas shoes. Afraid of getting sunburned, she had pulled her hands up into her sleeves and kept the towel over her head to cover her face.

She had rationed her water, belatedly realising that she had brought nowhere near enough water to meet her needs in such a challenging environment. Simultaneously she had asked herself what she had planned to do if she *had* miraculously found the airport. She had not thought through what she was trying to do. How could she have boarded a plane to go anywhere? She had no money, no identification, no phone, no passport, none of the necessities required for travel…

Now as she headed for the little triangle of shade she could see below the giant rocky outcrop, she was getting scared because she was down to her last inch of water in the bottle and, although she wasn't yet admitting it to herself, she knew she was lost because when she had, at one nervous point, attempted to retrace her steps she had discovered that the steadily building breeze had already covered them up, leaving her with no idea of which direction she had come from. Now her head was aching and she was getting cramps in her legs and resting until the heat at least eased off seemed the best option available.

She hated deserts because everything looked the same, she told herself fearfully as she slumped into the shade, and something with more legs than she cared to count scampered out of the gloom and sped off, as alarmed by her approach and startled cry as she was by its flight. She didn't like insects or snakes or lizards and she had already seen far too many such creatures to relax, having discovered that although the landscape looked reassuringly empty, that was a misconception. A whole host of nasty things lurked in unexpected places. She rocked back and forth, dimly appreciating that she was no longer quite firing on all mental cylinders and that she was unwell.

She had done the Djalians' work for them, she reflected dizzily. She had wandered off, got hopelessly lost and now she was going to die in the desert. She had another tiny sip of water, moistening her dry mouth while noticing that her arm had developed a sort of tremor that was unnerving.

Like Azrael—unnerving like Azrael. He had disturbed her, set off her temper and enraged her. It was *his* fault this had happened to her, *his* fault she had made such a dumb decision, she brooded, steeped in physical misery. She was hot, thirsty, dirty, sore and the tip of her nose hurt where the sun had got at it. The King, who had tried to buy her off.

Although the money *would* have come in useful, she acknowledged sleepily, her thoughts beginning to slow down, making her feel a little like a clock that badly needed winding up. Maurice would miss her visits, she thought, even if he couldn't tell her apart from the mother she barely even remembered. And she didn't mind that reality, no, of course she didn't, when her grandfather had been the only person who ever seemed to love her. Did that mean that *she* was just unlovable? She had often wondered that. Her father hadn't cared enough about her to protect her from his wife, while her stepmother had hated her almost on sight. Tahir had liked her in the wrong way, she reasoned in a daze, while Azrael… Why was she thinking about *him* again? Well, Azrael had hated her on sight too.

And then suddenly there was noise, the ground beneath her shifting as a horse galloped across the sand towards her. Poor horse, she thought numbly; if it was too hot for her, it had to be too hot for the horse as well. The horse, however, carried some sort of tribesman and she contrived to stretch out an arm and wave from the shade as though she were hailing a bus to stop for her.

The figure vaulted off the horse and the ground under her hips moved at the thump of booted feet.

'You stupid, *stupid* woman,' a familiar voice scolded.

And a weird kind of joyous relief engulfed Molly as she struggled to focus on those intense dark golden eyes, which were all that showed in the headdress he wore that covered his mouth as well. Azrael had found her and, instantly, she knew she would be all right.

Azrael was less confident because the storm was moving in fast in a threatening dark smudge, which he could already see on the horizon. The high winds had brought down the mast and his phone had not worked since his last call when he had phoned in to share that he had identified Molly's tracks. Now they were too far from the fortress to make it back ahead of the storm. How the hell had she got so far before he found her? She had travelled miles into the desert, through mile after mile of the most blazingly unwelcoming landscape on earth. And she had done it without adequate clothing or footwear and any of the many pieces of equipment that would have kept her comfortable and safe. She was crazy but she was also strong, Azrael acknowledged, squatting down to hand her a water bottle and grab it off her again before she made herself sick.

'Hands off, Mr Grumpy,' she told him with a giggle.

She was delirious from heat and thirst, Azrael interpreted in frustration. He lifted her and bundled her into a cloak, noting the red tip of her nose with a groan.

'What's wrong?' she slurred.

'You have burned your nose.'

'Do I look like Rudolph?'

'Who's Rudolph?' Azrael lifted her and draped her over his horse like a folded carpet. She was safe: he *had* found her. A little of the tension holding his powerful frame taut dissipated. He would take her to the cave and plunge her in the pool to cool her off. Hopefully by that stage the storm would have passed and they could be picked up. No aircraft could take off in such weather because it was too dangerous.

'Santa's reindeer,' Molly responded thickly, struggling to vocalise and think at the same time. ' I don't like you.'

'Keep quiet,' Azrael intoned flatly. 'Save your strength.'

What strength? Molly would have asked had she the power because she felt as floppy and as weak as a newborn and she hated the smell of horse. 'Horses stink.'

Azrael rolled his eyes and tugged on Spice's reins to head for the cave where he had hidden as a child with his mother from Hashem's soldiers. 'You didn't do too badly for a city girl,' he heard himself pronounce. 'It was an outstand-ingly stupid move, of course, but you travelled a great distance—'

'Shut up,' Molly moaned.

Azrael grinned. 'There's nothing I enjoy more than a trapped audience.'

'Butrus thinks you walk on water, O Glorious Leader,' she mumbled.

'I am an ordinary man,' Azrael countered with crushing calm.

Molly's eyes closed. *Ordinary?* Somehow she didn't think so. Mr Gorgeous had come after her and saved her and she was grateful even if he did annoy the hell out of her. She didn't mind that he had become Mr Grumpy again by the time he found her. 'Thanks,' she framed hoarsely.

And that was the last thing Molly remembered before she recovered consciousness in what felt like a freezing cold bath. Her eyes were heavy and gritty and opening them took as much effort as trying to lift her arms out of the water.

'No,' a familiar voice declared. 'You must stay in the water to cool your body down.'

She let her eyes stay closed because she thought she was dreaming. They had been in the desert where there was no water, certainly none he could submerge her entire body in. Her mind wandered off again and she drifted, only minimally aware of being roughly towelled, something catching at her ribcage and a yanking sensation before she was laid down somewhere, fabric of some kind lying lightly on her skin. She felt cool, wonderfully, blessedly cool for the first time in hours and she made no protest when she was lifted up and a bottle was put to her lips to drink. She gulped back the water and lay down again, her senses beginning to return to her. Her lashes lifted only a little because her eyes were so heavy and she had a blurred glimpse then of a man undressing.

She shouldn't look, a bossy little inner voice told her brain. She shut her eyes and breathed in deep, stifling that prissy voice, and she looked. And what she saw was a sight she was persuaded even at that moment that she would never forget... Azrael naked and an absolute symphony of bronzed, muscular male perfection from his wide, smooth brown shoulders, down the long, graceful golden line of his spine to his small, taut, masculine buttocks and his powerful hair-roughened thighs. A thick blue-black mane of hair brushed those amazing shoulders as well. She closed her eyes again fast, feeling like a shameless voyeur. She was perving on him when he thought himself unobserved, having assumed that she was asleep, and she should be ashamed of herself. She had never thought a man could be beautiful before and now she had learned different because, stripped of clothes, Azrael was magnificent.

Azrael slumped down into the chill of the cave pool with intense relief. His body had betrayed him as his mind could not. He was so turned on he literally hurt from the pounding pulse of his arousal. A man without ready access to sex should never, *ever* be forced to undress a woman, he reasoned in exasperation. He had removed only the dress, submerging her in the bra and panties she still wore, determined not to give Molly any reason to accuse him of overfamiliarity.

And then the blasted towel had caught on the

bra hook and ripped the heavy-duty bra half off, a garment more surely suited to an old and very sensible lady rather than a young and beautiful one. So, having partially detached and damaged the wretched thing, he had had to remove the bra, revealing the sort of bountiful pale curves topped by the most succulent nipples that any man would have... Azrael gritted his teeth, killing his thoughts stone dead, perspiration breaking on his brow. He was being thoroughly punished for his lack of physical control. But he had done what he had to do and she was safe and unharmed, he reminded himself soothingly. Now he should be able to relax...but relaxation had never been more of a challenge for him.

Molly wakened to a shadowed darkness that startled her as she gazed up at the craggy stone roof far above and realised that she was not in a building but in a very large cave. And then she saw the rusty old lantern glowing on the edge of the rock pool that she now appreciated must have illuminated that glimpse she'd had of Azrael naked. A small waterfall emerged directly from the rocks behind the pool and flowed down to break the still surface of the clear water. She blinked and sat up, remembering her experience in the desert with a shudder and acknowledging that, considering her earlier condition, she now felt astonishingly normal. She would have to thank Azrael. Had she thanked him? She wasn't sure. But he deserved thanks for defying her worst expectations and coming out into the desert to find her and rescue her. So, where was he?

She sat up, disconcerted to discover that her breasts were bare but relieved she was still wearing her knickers. She was lying on some sort of old rug that smelled a little musty and her dress had been laid over her like a sheet. In haste she pulled it on over her head and scrambled upright, extracting her hair and smoothing it down in an effort to control her curls. Only then when she turned her head did she see the flickering shadows at the far end of the cave where a small fire burned and a dark figure sat, his back turned to her. She hastened to shove her feet back into her sneakers.

As she trod over the sandy floor of the cave she became aware of a low rumbling sound and her brow pleated. 'What's that noise?' she asked.

'The sandstorm is moving in.' Azrael turned his head, his bold bronzed profile etched against the leaping flames. 'I *had* to find you before it hit and we can't return to the fortress until it's over.'

'Is a sandstorm that dangerous?'

'Some of them.' Azrael watched her move past him to head round the corner into the front section of the cavern, which was open to the elements. 'Don't try to go outside,' he warned her.

Molly nervously skirted the giant black stallion tethered there and headed for the dark entrance to stare out in consternation at the thick brown band on the skyline that was already blotting out the sun and making late afternoon dark as night. A strong wind plastered her dress back against her body and made it impossible to stand her ground and, even worse, there was dust on the wind. A horrible choking cloud of dust engulfed her, flying into her mouth and her eyes until she retreated hurriedly from her viewpoint.

'Couldn't you have warned me what it would be like out there?' Molly complained, shaking her hair and dress out to free them of dust and then wiping at her gritty face in disgust, grateful when Azrael passed her a water bottle.

Azrael, who had not put his head cloth back on, raised a satiric black brow at the question. 'Would you have listened to me? I think you prefer to reach your own conclusions.'

Molly pursed her lips in acknowledgement as she folded down on her knees on the other side of the fire. She knew she was stubborn, didn't need reminding of the fact and was well aware that she would never have ended up in her current predicament had she been of a more malleable disposition. 'I've had to rely on my own judgement for years,' she said defensively. 'I live alone.'

'You have no family?'

'No...well, I have my grandfather but he has dementia now and he's in a care home because he can't be left alone while I'm at work. My mother died when I was very young and my father, a few years ago,' she told him. 'And you? Any family apart from Tahir?'

'No parents alive either. I have Tahir's father, who was once my stepfather, but it is not a family relationship since my mother's death. I try, however, to maintain good relations with him because his country is on our border,' he admitted bluntly. 'And sometimes it is a struggle to maintain even that because his outlook differs so much from mine.'

'In what way?' Molly questioned curiously.

'Quarein has lately cracked down on the freedoms of their minorities and some of those affected have fled over the border to claim refugee status here in Djalia. Despite his many other sins, the former dictator did not persecute minorities,' Azrael explained with a wry quirk of his sculpted lips. 'Sadly, Tahir's father, Prince Firuz, fiercely disapproves of Djalian tolerance, but it is what my people want, and when I took the throne I promised to protect the freedoms of *all* Djalian citizens. Our refugees fall into the same category.'

'I think being all-inclusive is good,' Molly said thoughtfully.

'But that has costs as well,' Azrael pointed out ruefully. 'Every decision leads to a reaction, and not always the one I want or expect.'

'So, being a king isn't all rainbows and kittens?' Molly quipped.

'No, it's hard work and no fun,' Azrael admitted grimly. 'And I worry constantly about making a mistake that could damage my country.'

'And then Tahir kidnapped me and dropped you in it,' Molly commented softly, strangely touched by his honesty about what it was really like to be a glorious leader.

Looking very sombre, Azrael nodded. In the firelight, his black hair had the glossy, iridescent sheen of a raven's wing, feathering round his shoulders, framing that beautiful face of his, his cheekbones smooth cut and sharp as bronzed blades. But he was so serious, so incredibly serious, Molly registered with intense frustration. If he had a lighter side to his nature, he never showed it and she had yet to see him smile.

'Smile...' she urged helplessly.

'Why?' Azrael asked baldly. 'There is nothing to smile about.'

Molly laughed, easy humour tilting her full lips into a helpless grin. 'You can be such a misery. But look at us... I would have died out there if you hadn't found me. And you rescued me, for which I shall be grateful for ever. I'm fine, you're fine, we're both safe...even cosy,' she selected, indicating the leaping flames of the little fire with a playful gesture. 'You've got plenty to smile about now.'

'Are you grateful enough to drop the idea of prosecuting my brother?' Azrael shot at her, fighting the disturbing truth that her easy grin was captivating and made her eyes sparkle while the reflection of the flames picked out amazing rich copper tones in her wonderful hair. He could not afford to be sidetracked by his natural male instincts.

Her grin immediately died. 'I'm sorry, no... and that wasn't a fair question. I thought we were talking off the record and I let my guard down...

I was trying to be friendly,' she extended uncomfortably.

'I'm *never* off the record,' Azrael admitted flatly, while on another level he was trying to suppress he was wondering exactly what 'friendliness' encompassed in her parlance.

During his six short months in London the year before, he had met women who offered him sex as casually as a handshake and as freely as if he were offering a workout at the gym. It had been a learning experience that had sent him from initially shocked to ecstatic and, finally and surprisingly, to a kind of repugnance he couldn't adequately explain. He didn't know whether it was his upbringing or some innate conservative streak somewhere inside him, but he had discovered that careless intimacy was a challenge for him. That was why he had considered getting married. But marriage would bring other difficulties and he thought he had enough to deal with without inviting more problems into his already very demanding life.

'That's unhealthy,' Molly told him without hesitation.

'No, it is a fact,' Azrael shot back at her coolly.
'I am who I am and I can't change that or step
back from it when it suits me. Everything I do
reflects on my status and I will be judged for it.'

Molly tossed her head in dismissal. Her copper ringlets danced round her flushed cheeks,
her temper beginning to spark in the face of his
relentless gravity. 'I'll be honest too, then. I very
much resent your continuing apprehension on
your brother's behalf. I didn't ask to be in this
situation. He *put* me in it and he *planned* the kidnapping, which is even worse,' she argued.

Even before she had finished speaking, Azrael
unfolded with angry speed from his seat on the
sand. He moved so fast that she blinked, her attention unerringly caught by the seamless silent
grace and tightly coiled energy that was so much
a part of him. 'We will not argue about that matter here and now,' he stated, staring down at her
with engrained arrogance.

But Molly refused to be diverted. She had to

plant her hands on the sand to rise upright again and it felt clumsy because she was ridiculously conscious of how much less agile she was in comparison with him. 'I will argue with you if I want to,' she responded, wishing that statement didn't sound slightly childish to her own ears even if it was what he needed to hear.

Azrael stalked down the length of the cave to grasp the lantern and carry it over the saddle bags resting by the wall. Molly was helplessly entranced by his fluid movements because he flowed like water without making a sound, while his perfect hawkish profile was etched in shadow against the wall.

'Are you going to ignore me now?' Molly prompted helplessly.

'I am not in the mood for another…dispute,' he framed impatiently. 'Particularly not while we are stuck together in this cave for the duration of the storm.'

Her teeth gritted together. 'I would prefer to clear the air.'

'We cannot clear the air unless you are willing

to compromise,' Azrael fired back at her, stalking back towards her, all seething masculine energy and soundless grace, dark eyes glittering a warning in the subdued light.

'Why should *I* be willing to compromise?' Molly demanded stormily, for throughout her childhood and adolescence she had been forced to make continual compromises. Unpleasant realities had limited her and removed her choices. She hadn't been able to change the truths that her mother was dead, her father was indifferent and her stepmother disliked and mistreated her. As soon as she had attained adulthood and independence she had sworn never to be forced into compromises again and to put her own wants and wishes first. These days only Maurice's needs came before her own.

'Have an energy bar while you're thinking about it,' Azrael urged, dropping one into her hand, long brown fingers briefly brushing her palm, sending the strangest frisson of awareness travelling through her unprepared body.

Involuntarily she collided with his smouldering

dark gaze and it was as if fireworks broke out inside her, magnifying the leap of heat low in her pelvis that made her breasts tighten and her nipples peak. It unnerved her because she had never felt that way before and instantly she wanted to back away from him. It was attraction, of course, she realised that, but feeling that way even when she was angry with him unsettled her because she had always assumed that anger would be a defence against feeling anything she didn't want to feel. Eager to lose that uncomfortable awareness of him, she turned hurriedly away and tore open the energy bar. Out of the corner of her eye as she ate she watched Azrael lead the horse to the pool, where it noisily drank its fill.

'What do you call him?'

'Spice.' Azrael smoothed the stallion's flank in a gesture of affection. 'He is the best horse in my stable.'

'I've never been this close to a horse before,' Molly admitted. 'I grew up in the country though. There were horses in the field next to the house but I was too nervous of them to get close.'

'Come here…and meet him,' Azrael urged, extending a long-fingered brown hand in a fluid invitation.

'I'd really rather not.'

Azrael studied her in astonishment. 'And yet you walked out into the desert without fear?'

'That was different. Ignorance was bliss. I didn't know what it would really be like. I've never even been abroad before,' Molly heard herself confide as her feet moved her closer because, as soon as Azrael had recognised her fear, her pride had come into play and forced her forward.

'Never? You've *never* visited another country?' Azrael queried in amazement, for he had always assumed that in an era of cheap travel *all* Western people travelled widely.

'I could never afford to travel,' Molly advanced reluctantly. 'It's always been at the top of my wish list, though, but necessities come first, you know…although I suppose you *don't* know what I'm talking about, given the wealth Tahir seemed determined to splash in my direction.'

'Unlike his, my life has not always been one

of wealth, comfort and security. Perhaps, had he had my experiences, he might have grown up a little faster than he has. For many months, when my mother and I were being hunted, we lived in this cave—'

'You lived...*here*?' she pressed in astonishment. 'You were hunted? By whom?'

'Hashem. He had executed my father and he wanted to remove me from my mother's care. She lived here in very trying conditions for *my* benefit, a princess who had never known hardship in her life,' he explained heavily. 'She could have gone home to her family in Quarein but she was afraid that the man who was then ruling Quarein would insist on handing me over to Hashem.'

'What age were you?' Molly exclaimed, shaken by what she was learning about his past because it lay so far outside her naïve expectations.

'Ten years old.' Azrael had never before had to explain his background to anyone because all his people naturally knew his history, and he wondered why he was confiding in her. Was it the magnetic warmth of compassion in her eyes and her dismay on his behalf? He questioned why her reaction should break through his usual innate reserve.

'Ten?' Molly gasped helplessly. 'What sort of horrible person would even consider handing over a *child* to the man who had executed his father?'

Azrael swallowed hard, for he was even less used to having to admit the relationship that had weighed him down with shame from birth. 'Hashem was my father's father, my grandfather, and had he sworn not to harm me his claim to me would have been acknowledged because after my father's death, I became Hashem's heir.'

Molly was poleaxed as she put those facts together. 'Your grandfather executed his own son?' she whispered in horror.

Azrael's chin lifted in a grim nod of acknowledgement. 'My father led the rebel forces before me,' he proffered in a harsh undertone, emotion unconcealed in the flare of his nostrils and the narrowing of his amazing gold-tinted eyes. 'But twenty years ago those forces were not strong enough to depose Hashem and the coup failed.'

'And your father paid with his life,' Molly completed for herself.

'Out of respect for him and the many who died at Hashem's hands, we prefer to refer to him as the *dictator*, rather than the King,' Azrael completed, using the opportunity to clasp her hand and draw it down gently over Spice's smooth, warm neck. 'Hashem tarnished the throne with his hunger for absolute power.'

'But your people obviously don't hold that against you or you wouldn't be King now,' Molly said for herself, taken aback when the horse nudged her shoulder, evidently enjoying her attention and wanting more of it.

'I must always be careful not to betray their trust.'

And an international scandal unleashed by the King's half-brother could well cause a lot of trouble, Molly found herself thinking with regret, and then she was annoyed with herself for thinking along such lines. After all, she was British, not Djalian, and Azrael's dysfunctional family history should have no bearing on her righteous wrath over what Tahir had done to her. She petted the horse, striving to suppress a fresh leap of anger at her predicament.

'I could've had an adverse reaction to that drug Tahir used on me and been injured. Many things could have gone wrong,' she pointed out.

'But luckily they didn't,' Azrael interposed softly.

'I'm afraid I still want Tahir to face the full consequences of what he did,' Molly murmured thinly.

'I would agree if he were an adult, but he's not.'

Molly's brow furrowed, her eyes widening. 'What do you mean…he's *not* an adult? Of course, he is! How old is he? Twenty-two? Twenty-three?'

Azrael stared back at her, his stunning dark golden eyes frowning at her question. 'I assumed that you knew his age. How could you mistake Tahir for an adult? My brother is sixteen years old—'

'*Sixteen?*' Molly yelped in rampant disbelief as she whirled away from the horse. 'You can't be serious! I was kidnapped by a *teenager*?'

'You really didn't know,' Azrael registered in wonderment as he scanned her incredulous face.

'Of course, I didn't know!' Molly rounded furiously on him with that admission as she crossed the sand on restive feet. 'I tried to find out his age at the first lesson but he was evasive and his English was poor. I was afraid I was getting too personal and being rude, so I let it go. Sixteen, though...my goodness, he's a giant for sixteen!'

'Perhaps, but he is not particularly mature,' Azrael remarked. 'Surely you noticed that, at least?'

Molly bridled at the faint edge of scorn to that question. 'Well, yes, I did notice but I was very aware that he was from a different culture and I don't know what's normal for young men in your society.'

'We are people, exactly the same as you!' Azrael lanced back at her with simmering irritation.

'Oh, for goodness' sake, what I'm trying to say is that, yes, I *did* notice that he was immature but I kind of blamed that on his upbringing and his not having any experience of my world,' Molly expanded, refusing to rise to the bait of his annoyance. 'I am not prejudiced in any way, Azrael.'

'If that is so, I am glad to hear it,' Azrael conceded, his wide, sensual mouth compressed. 'Unfortunately for all of us, my brother gave no prior sign of the insane thing he did to you. Tahir is an average boy. He spends hours playing computer games and he's mad about cars and girls.'

'And he kidnaps his English teacher, who is almost seven years older than him! No way is that typical!' Molly shot back at him fierily and she spun away from him, exasperated beyond bearing by his arguments.

'No, it is not typical,' Azrael admitted grudgingly. 'But I cannot help but blame myself for not taking more of an interest in him. It is unlucky that he is so much younger and that I have been so preoccupied here. Our mother died last year and it hit him very hard—'

'I refuse to listen to a sob story on Tahir's behalf!' Molly flung back at Azrael in frustration, her eyes bright with mounting fury. 'That is not fair to me. Why should I consider Tahir's state of mind when he did not consider what he was doing to me?'

'I said that we should not discuss this here,' Azrael responded icily. 'I do not want you shouting at me.'

Molly's hands knotted into fists. She watched Spice sidle back out to the front of the cave, presumably as spooked as his owner by her loud voice, and then turned back to scrutinise Azrael's lean, darkly handsome but undeniably frozen features. She was darned if she was going to apologise, most particularly not when it felt amazing to not care about the impression she was making and to speak her mind freely. After all, growing up she had been deprived of that freedom far too often. Forced to fit in with other people's expectations, she had had to try to placate her stepmother simply in the hope of gaining peace. But appeasement hadn't got her very far and hadn't made the older woman any kinder.

'My emotions don't come with volume control,' she confessed tightly. 'And I am not usually this emotional but the past forty-eight hours have been very upsetting for me and I'm on edge, which means my temper is on edge too.'

Almost imperceptibly, Azrael's lean, powerful frame became a little less rigid. 'Obviously I can understand that but I cannot tolerate shouting.'

Molly sucked in a steadying breath, dismayed by the realisation that the more he prohibited her natural behaviour, the more he simply made her want to shout. There was something very basic in her, she sensed, that literally *had* to fight Azrael's dominance and, inexplicably, when she spoke her mind to him in anger, she felt as if she was finally being herself and was unashamed of the fact. 'And I cannot tolerate being told that I can't shout,' she confided guiltily. 'Yet I very rarely do it. Obviously *you* make me angry and aggressive—'

And without the smallest warning, Azrael smiled and it illuminated his serious features like a sudden flash of sunlight, firing up the gold in his eyes enhanced by his ridiculously thick black lashes, accentuating his exotic cheekbones, revealing even white teeth and a wonderfully shapely mouth. That charismatic smile made him so handsome that her heart jumped inside her and her tummy dropped as though she had gone down in a lift too fast. She was startled; her mouth ran dry and her breath caught in her throat.

'So, it's *my* fault that you shout,' Azrael derided silkily in a tone she had never heard from him before.

'Yes,' Molly replied squarely. 'I find you extremely annoying. You try to tell me what to do. You patronise me. Then you freeze if I get annoyed…but you're the one *making* me annoyed!'

Azrael paced closer as silent as a stalking cat on the trail of prey. 'I don't annoy other people—'

'And I don't shout at anyone else,' Molly interposed.

'Perhaps you are focusing your anger with Tahir on me,' Azrael suggested.

'No!' Molly disagreed, reluctant to acknowledge that she could possibly be that unaware of her own responses. 'But why did nobody *tell* me that I was teaching a teenager? Looking at him,

I'd never have guessed that he was still only a boy. Someone should have told me what age he was.'

Azrael lifted a fine ebony brow. 'Or you should have asked one of the embassy staff.'

'I had no reason to suspect he was that young and I'm not sure it changes anything.' Molly looped a long coppery rope of curls back from her hot face and glowered at Azrael accusingly. 'Why *should* it change anything? It was a grown-up crime,' she blustered, not knowing what she planned to do or how she felt about the unexpected fact she had just learned.

But the fact of the matter was that occasionally teenagers *did* do crazy things and, ironically, nobody knew that better than Molly. At the age of fourteen, Molly had packed her bag and run away from her family home. She had planned to go to London to become a musician in a band, for goodness' sake. Sadly, the cost of the train fare had thwarted that fanciful ambition and in a rage of tempestuous teenage fury she had landed on Maurice's doorstep, where he had talked some sense back into her.

Maurice had returned her to her father's home and when she had seen her, her stepmother had said angrily, 'I *knew* it was too good to be true. I *knew* you'd come back again!'

And then her father and Maurice had had an argument, for which she had also received the blame. Her slight shoulders drooped at her distressing recollection of that day. That was the moment that she knew that she would not approach the police in London about what Tahir had done. He was sixteen and, while she couldn't forgive him for the fright he had given her and the risk he had taken with her health, she knew that teenagers could make stupid decisions and fatal mistakes and she realised that she no longer wanted him to pay the full adult price for his wrongdoing.

In addition, if she went to the police about what Tahir had done, it would inevitably attract the interest of the press and she didn't want her name and her face splashed across the newspapers or people speculating about whether or not she might have encouraged Tahir in his delusions. Nor would the subsequent scandal improve her employment prospects. No, there would be no benefit to her in making an official complaint.

Abstractedly, she studied Azrael, guessing that he had probably been a very sensible teenager with an outlook older than his years. 'You never did tell me how far we are out here from the airport.'

'Several hundred miles,' Azrael murmured, his attention welded to the tender fullness of her naturally pink lips while he inevitably wondered if they would taste as soft and lush as they looked.

Her green eyes flew wide. 'Several *hundred*?' she repeated in disbelief, clashing with shimmering dark golden eyes that made her feel oddly light-headed and even more oddly detached from her brain. 'But how did you get me to the fortress yesterday?'

'By helicopter, of course,' Azrael explained. 'We fly in and out. The cars pick us up at the landing site and drive us the rest of the way—'

'But there must be a road somewhere nearby—'

'No. Beyond the oil fields we do not yet have a country-wide network of roads, nor will we have until our construction engineers embark on that project,' Azrael admitted, faint colour lining his sculpted cheekbones. 'This part of the desert has always been fairly inaccessible.'

Molly experienced a sudden startling desire to smooth her fingers gently across one of those exotic cheekbones and so foreign was that forbidden prompting that her face began to flush as she questioned it. She had never before wanted to touch a man of her own volition. Her fingers fluttered and her nails bit into her palms, her breathing struggling in the new tightness of her chest. A kind of craving was snaking through her like a wildfire that burned everything that stood before it, and it shook her because that craving was so powerful it swallowed all common sense.

A drumming boom sounded outside the cave and she flinched.

'It is only the storm,' Azrael breathed tautly when a crashing roar seemed to shake the very rock walls of the cavern protecting them.

'I would have hated being caught outside in that,' Molly admitted shakily, ultra-conscious of the smouldering silence enclosing them and speaking in a deliberate attempt to shatter an atmosphere that was becoming suffocating. 'I didn't realise it would be so violent.'

'The elements in our climate are often violent and perverse,' Azrael declared huskily, reaching for her hand and tugging her closer, knowing that what he was doing was wrong but utterly unable to continue battling the urge to touch her. 'Just as you make me feel things I don't want to feel…'

Her hand engulfed in his, Molly looked up at him, knowing she should back away, knowing that she should be listening to the voice of reason inside her head. But that close to Azrael she couldn't think, she could only *feel*. And what she felt just then was the incredibly seductive sensation of being thrillingly alive, her heart thumping fast while adrenalin raced in her veins.

'Tell me not to touch you,' Azrael urged thickly, brilliant dark deep-set eyes shimmering like gold ingots across her hectically flushed face.

CHAPTER FOUR

AND MOLLY COULDN'T tell Azrael that because
she didn't want to. Even the innocent word, touch,
awakened a storm of seething curiosity and volatile awareness inside her. Her body felt as primed
as though a detonator were ready to set it off. She
was on the very edge of that fierce craving and,
without the smallest hesitation, her hands came
up to reach into the front of his robe to bring him
closer.

That fast Azrael's mouth came down hard on
hers, driving her lips apart for the savage plunge
of his tongue. Molly shuddered, excitement leaping high as flames flared inside her, the hot li-
quidity at the heart of her swiftly becoming a
burning, unbearable ache. Within seconds she
wanted more than she had ever wanted before in
a man's arms and she was locked to every long,

virile line of him on tiptoe, her hands lacing into the silky depths of his luxuriant black hair. More, more, *more*, her body seemed to scream with single-minded purpose as the raw hunger threatened to consume her. She couldn't breathe, she couldn't think of anything but her instinctive fear that he would let her go.

Azrael tried to let her go but because he had supressed the attraction so hard one tiny taste of Molly's yielding mouth unleashed a ferocious surge of lust. He was utterly aroused, throbbing close to the edge of pain. She was plastered to him so that he could feel every soft feminine curve but it was nowhere near enough to satisfy his hunger. Her lips were open but he wanted *all* of her open. He wanted her spread under him naked and eager. He wanted to surge into the warm, wet welcome of her body and sate the need riding him as hard as the storm outside rode the land.

He lifted her high against him, her hands dropping to clutch at his shoulders for support. 'I want you, *aziz*,' he growled, settling her down on the worn Persian rug that she had slept on earlier.

And Molly wanted him as she had never wanted a man before. She was already wondering if such strong feelings were what she had always subconsciously waited and hoped to find. Outside the storm rumbled while, inside her, her heart thudded and raced and she angled up ecstatically to the sudden welcome weight of Azrael's body as he ground down on her. The piercingly sweet, sharp arousal thrumming through her pelvis was unbearable.

He was crushing her mouth and she revelled in his urgency, tiny little flickers of excitement dancing through her wherever his body melded to hers. The plunge of his tongue into the warm, wet interior of her mouth sent a pulse of ferocious heat right down to the very heart of her. He was yanking up her dress and she made no protest because for the first time she too hungered for touch. In any case, she felt safe with Azrael, knew he would stop if she asked, somehow knew he would do nothing that she didn't want.

Baring the soft ripe swell of her creamy breasts, Azrael was enraptured by her. There were so many possibilities that he hardly knew where to begin until the jutting prominence of a rosy nipple took precedence. He stroked that straining nub with a reverent fingertip.

'You are so beautiful,' he told her in Arabic. 'So...*perfect*.'

And for once there was no thought of tomorrow or even what he was doing in Azrael's usually very organised brain. He could do nothing but claim her luscious mouth again while his eager hands explored the warm, heavy weight of her silken breasts, skimming the pouting peaks with teasing fingers while she twisted and moaned under him, as impatient as he was for something to satisfy the craving that controlled them both.

An agonised gasp escaped Molly as Azrael eased between her thighs and moved against the most achingly sensitive part of her entire body. She arched up to him, wanting, *needing*. Was this it? Was this finally the moment when she would take the plunge? she was wondering helplessly. In the back of her mind, she was surprisingly calm, reminding herself that she was on the pill, not only to regulate her menstrual cycle, but also to ensure that she never ran the risk of an unplanned pregnancy.

Azrael's lips engulfed a velvety pink nipple and suckled. Her spine arched, a startled moan wrenched from her parted lips. Every tiny sound of pleasure that escaped her ramped his desire higher still. Her lips tasted as ripe as fresh strawberries, Azrael decided, gazing down at her through the thick veil of his lashes in awe, revelling in her responsiveness. Long brown fingers skimmed down to skate over the stretched taut triangle of fabric between her legs, recognising the heat and moisture there, moving to uncover it and then freezing as a dilemma he had never thought to face gripped him. Birth control…and he had nothing. Teeth gritting, Azrael yanked his burning body back from her and rolled off her, a curse of frustration forming on his tongue and swallowed back with the steely control that was so much a part of him.

'Azrael…?' Molly framed uncertainly, lifting her tousled head.

'We cannot continue. I have no contraception,' he breathed in a raw undertone.

Dazed, Molly sat up, her entire body leaping and throbbing with a pulsing excitement that had yet to drain away. In some ways she was in shock because she knew she had been on the brink of giving up her virginity in the equivalent of a one-night stand. Logic and practicality warned her that she could never have anything more with a reigning king. She also recognised that for the first time ever she had met with pure sexual temptation and she had succumbed so fast to its allure that she was shattered. Even at that instant, acknowledging that she had not known what she was doing even while she *thought* that she did, she was tempted to part her lips and assure him that there was no risk of pregnancy because she was taking contraception.

But before she could speak she asked herself when she had last taken a pill and dismay swept her because she kept her pills in her handbag and she had not seen her bag since before she was kidnapped. Her bag had probably been left behind in the Djalian Embassy in London and she had missed a couple of pills and was no longer protected. Why hadn't she thought of that reality sooner? Because it hadn't occurred to her that a kiss could lead to so much *more*…

'It is not a risk I can take,' Azrael breathed tautly.

'Of course not,' Molly agreed circumspectly, her face burning like mad as she wondered what the source of Azrael's fatal attraction was. He was gorgeous, yes, she accepted that…and when he touched her it was as if the whole world erupted in flames and suddenly she hadn't cared about anything or anybody. For the space of a few crazy minutes, her body had controlled her, *he* had controlled her. Shock slivered through her because all her common sense had gone straight out of the window. She wasn't a prude, she told herself, but she had always assumed that she would be in a relationship when she finally had sex with someone. That would have been a measured, *sensible* decision.

Yanking her dress down, Molly scrambled upright, refusing to look at Azrael. Her legs felt like cotton wool and outside the storm was still ominously rumbling. Another pressing need took charge of her enervated body and she said stiltedly, 'I'm going to have to go outside…'

Azrael strode over to the edge of the pool to lift the rusty lantern and returned to her. 'There is no need,' he told her, planting a guiding hand to her spine to lead her to the very back of the cave where a large rock concealed a narrow fissure in the craggy wall. 'The facilities are primitive but adequate,' he informed her.

And even by the dull light of the lantern she could see that the facilities were rudimentary but she was so grateful to see them, she smiled in relief, realising that the amenity of crude indoor plumbing had to date back to Azrael's stay with his mother in the cave. Necessity taken care of and her hands tingling with the chill of a wash in cold water, she returned to the main cave and wandered back to the fire, striving not to be self-conscious. After all, they had got a little carried away but really nothing very much had happened. Ultimately good sense had stopped them in their tracks.

Azrael was staring steadily into the fire, striving for calm and cool while his essentially volatile nature warred with conflicting urges below the surface. He had never wanted anything as much as he had wanted to sate himself on her fiery passion. Denied that outlet and, indeed, *any* prospect of relief, he seethed inside himself like a cauldron bubbling on a fire. He ached with arousal and frustration and regret.

Molly dropped down opposite and ruefully studied his brooding dark features. 'You're like a wet weekend, Azrael. Lighten up. We got a little silly but nothing happened.'

His beautifully moulded mouth compressed. 'We will not discuss it.'

Molly collided with brilliant dark golden eyes and a flock of butterflies took off in her stomach again and she almost groaned. That wretched attraction wouldn't go away, wouldn't quit making itself heard and felt, but just then she didn't want that awareness of him. Yet she could remember times when she had actually longed to feel the powerful pull of sex that she had heard other women describe. So, now she knew that, after all, she was normal and in possession of all the usual hormones and drives, she told herself impatiently. Just her luck that only a desert king had the power to affect her that way and that it had been a once-in-a-lifetime experience.

'I could talk out loud and you could choose not to listen,' she suggested facetiously.

Black lashes lifted to reveal impatient, dark-as-night eyes shorn of shimmering gold. 'We will behave like adults.'

'Unfortunately I only want to push you fully dressed into the pool when you talk like that,' Molly admitted truthfully, scrambling upright again to go and investigate the storm. Push him in the pool and slap him, her brain added in exasperation. Did Azrael monitor and squash every human response? Did he always have to be in control? Was that why he was angry? Had he come too close to losing control with her?

The drumming, hissing roar of the continuing

storm took Molly aback. There was no sign that the storm was abating while the force of the wind almost sent her off her feet as well as coating her with fresh dust. Shaking herself irritably, she returned to the fire.

'Will it make you feel better if I tell you that I will *not* go to the police when I get back to London?' Molly asked drily.

Azrael slung her a narrowed questioning glance. 'What changed your mind? I thought you wanted justice.'

'I do but sometimes you have to take a rain check on what you want and opt for a proportionate response instead. Tahir did something crazy but I did something crazy too when I was a teenager. I didn't break the law but it did make me aware that I was not as mature as I thought I was at the time,' Molly told him flatly.

Curiosity infiltrated Azrael. 'What did you do?'

'I was only fourteen but I was convinced that I could become a professional musician and I ran away from home. I planned to go to London and lose myself before embracing fame,' she confided with a rueful grimace at the naivety of that dream, built entirely on the back of the small fact that she was a good pianist.

'Why?' he asked simply.

Molly swallowed hard, reluctant to share more. 'My stepmother was hurting me and it was getting worse.'

Azrael was frowning. 'How was she hurting you?' he demanded.

'She'd pinch me and pull my hair and slap my face and although I told my father, he wouldn't do anything about it. She said that I was cheeky but I wasn't. I had long since learned to keep quiet around her and try not to annoy her but it didn't change anything,' she confided ruefully. 'In the end, I went to live with my grandfather and I never saw my dad again. He didn't stay in touch.'

Azrael was listening, watching her with dark liquid deep-set eyes that glittered in the firelight. 'That is sad. Although my father died when I was only a boy I was very close to him.'

'At least you have some happy memories. Mine

are all of times with my grandfather,' Molly told him. 'I was very lucky that I had him to support me.'

'His illness must distress you.'

Molly shrugged a slim shoulder. 'I'm used to it now and I'm grateful to still have him alive. He's the only family I've got left.'

Azrael studied her with brooding force, admiring the clarity of her green eyes in her flushed heart-shaped face. 'Were you serious when you said you would not be pressing charges against Tahir?' he prompted.

Molly shook her head and groaned out loud. 'Are you *always* so distrustful? So suspicious? So reluctant to accept good news?'

'It's bred in the bone,' Azrael admitted without apology.

'It's unhealthy,' Molly contradicted.

'If you *are* serious, I thank you for your restraint and generosity.'

'It's not generosity, Azrael,' Molly countered with a wince. 'I'm afraid I haven't forgiven him. I just feel that having a teenager prosecuted for such a crime would be overkill. He probably thought he knew what he was doing but he didn't, and he didn't consider the future either. I've been there. I've done that. And as you said, I wasn't harmed.'

'Obviously you will be compensated for your kindness,' Azrael slotted in smoothly, disliking the conviction that he owed her a debt for her change of heart on his brother's behalf.

And that assurance was the last straw for Molly in the emotional mood she was in. She reared up in a temper. 'I didn't change my mind for the money!' she proclaimed furiously. 'Is that what you think? Obviously, that's what you think! Well, you're wrong, Azrael, totally, absolutely wrong!'

'You're shouting again,' Azrael remarked chillingly. 'Shouting is rude and unnecessary.'

'Oh, go to hell!' Molly launched back at him, out of all patience and stomping down the cave towards the rug that lay on the sand. 'I'm going to sleep. Wake me when we're being rescued! Otherwise, please forget I'm here!'

CHAPTER FIVE

AZRAEL GRITTED HIS teeth and watched Molly shiver while she slept. Never had he met such a hot-tempered woman. She went off like a rocket every time he offended her. She had gone off like a rocket in his arms as well, he recalled helplessly, his aching body hardening in enthusiastic recollection of her soft, silky skin and gloriously inviting mouth. In angry denial of that weakness, he stalked down the length of the cave and covered her with the cloak he had wrapped her in earlier.

Naturally he had assumed that the offer of financial compensation had slowly worked on her to change her mind. What else was he supposed to think? Now instead of feeling relief that Djalia was safe from a huge international scandal, he was in a rage. What was it about her that aggravated him to such an extent? Made him stumble into tactless speech and assumptions? He, the consummate diplomat, who had learned to watch every word he spoke from an early age! But he was no diplomat in Molly's radius. She got under his skin. She infuriated him but she was also incredibly exciting. He had never experienced that livewire connection with a woman before. He dredged his eyes from her slight figure in frustration and looked longingly at the pool, which would give his overheated body the coolness he craved.

With a wary eye in her direction he stripped and bathed for the second time that day. She might be cold but he was much too hot and the dust clogging the air and falling on every surface made him feel unclean. Freshened up, he unrolled his bedding by the fire and with a suppressed groan stalked down to check on his guest again. He touched her hand and it felt like ice and he swore under his breath. Taking a deep breath, he bent down and lifted her, praying that she wouldn't wake and assume that he was making some kind of sexual approach when his sole concern was that if she got any colder she might develop pneumonia or some such thing. She weighed very little, which he thought was a sign of fragility and unhealthiness. No wonder she was feeling the cold so badly. Keeping her wrapped in the cloak, he lay down with her and almost groaned again. Once she recovered her body heat, she would make him too warm.

Molly stirred, aware of the hard ground below her hip and the furnace-like heat at her back that made her feel deliciously cosy. She curled back into that reassuring warmth with a drowsy sigh.

'Be still. It is not yet dawn,' a familiar voice intoned, far too close for comfort.

'Azrael?' she squeaked in consternation.

'Who else?'

'Well, I don't know, do I?' Molly snapped defensively. 'I went to sleep *alone.*'

'You were shivering with cold. I had to do something.'

Stiff as a block of wood, Molly rolled her eyes in the dimness and shifted position.

'Stop moving about. You'll keep me awake,'

Azrael complained, already aching from the effects of a warm, curvy woman moving against his groin.

Well, at least she didn't need to worry that he was about to make a pass at her, Molly thought sourly. He was more concerned with getting back to sleep, but her eyes widened as he shifted and she recognised the hard thrust of his arousal against her bottom.

'Sorry, I'm not used to sleeping with anyone,' she mumbled, hot-faced at what even she knew to be a natural morning condition for a man.

Azrael thought about that. 'How is that possible?' he queried in audible surprise.

And that fast Molly wanted to slap him again.

'And you suggested that *I* might be prejudiced?' Molly scoffed helplessly. 'Forget about all those well-worn clichés you've heard about Western women. Like many others, I don't sleep around.'

'You don't have to sleep around to be accustomed to sharing a bed,' Azrael countered.

'Don't know what you mean by that,' Molly framed drowsily lacking in comprehension because she was deciding that the heat he provided definitely overruled his unfortunate personality. 'But I'm still a virgin.'

And with that simple statement, she stunned Azrael into silence. Was it possible? He lifted his tousled dark head to look down at her and a faint sleepy snore escaped her, proving that if she had said it for effect she wasn't staying awake to see if it had worked. He blinked, long black lashes fanning back down as he settled back again. He was *not* prejudiced, he reasoned fiercely. But it was possible that the casually sexual women who had entertained him in the past had somewhat skewed his expectations, he conceded thoughtfully. A virgin. And Tahir had kidnapped her! It was little wonder that she had been so shattered by her ordeal. Azrael removed the hand he had resting on her hip and backed off from direct contact. His aroused body screamed a protest but he studiously ignored it, his handsome mouth set in a rigid line. Once again, after all, he had been guilty of an assumption that had been an insult.

* * *

Molly was roughly shaken awake and urged to tidy up. She scrambled up, eyes alighting on Azrael, who was pacing and muttering.

'What on earth?' she began in bewilderment, her brow pleating as she heard the racket of helicopter rotor blades and raised voices.

Azrael held his fingers to his mouth in the universal silencing gesture. 'There are soldiers outside the cave,' he told her at low pitch. 'We are being rescued.'

'That's wonderful…why are you being *so*—?'

Teeth visibly gritting, Azrael strode towards her. 'Because the Djalian council declared an emergency and organised a totally unnecessary search for me, which in turn created a nationwide panic. Now there are journalists waiting outside and far too much interest in our plight has been stirred up,' he ground out in exasperation.

'OK…' Molly dragged out the acknowledgement reflectively and quite unthinkingly reached up to twitch his wildly tousled black hair back into some sort of order, belatedly recognising where the greyish film that rose in the air came from. 'You're covered in dust—'

Azrael caught her fluttering fingers in his. 'You will not speak when we go outside. I will handle everything...'

'Relax,' Molly urged him gently, believing that she understood the source of his apprehension. 'I have no intention of saying anything about Tahir. His name won't cross my lips—'

'*Nothing* must cross your lips,' Azrael told her tautly, wondering if she was always so naïve while cursing his brother and the predicament he had put them both in.

It did not seem to occur to her that if they could not tell the truth about *why* she was in Djalia, they would both be plunged into a maelstrom of demeaning conjecture. Azrael had never been publicly associated with any woman and he and Molly had spent the night alone in a cave. He could already hear Molly dismissing that reality as trivial and marvelling that anyone could possibly be interested in such a fact. Azrael, however, was less naïve. He knew his people would assume that Molly had been staying at the fortress with him because she was his secret lover, and nobody would be that shocked that he had a lover because he was a single man.

But, even so, it would still be unthinkable for him to stand back in silence while Molly's reputation was tarnished for ever by speculation that she was his mistress. Had Molly not, through no fault of her own, already suffered enough? Tahir had brought her to Djalia without her permission and Azrael had refused to let her go home. That was the only reason she had fled into the desert where she had almost died. Azrael lifted his arrogant dark head high, secure in the conviction that he was a king who *did* know right from wrong and that he did take responsibility for his mistakes. It was *his* duty to protect Molly from the consequences of Tahir's insanity and his own misjudgement.

And there was only one way to achieve that feat. For the first time in his life he would tell a lie to his people, he reflected grimly, but it would be a relatively harmless lie that would pull a mantle of respectability over their predicament. And by the mere voicing of that single lie, all the sleazy speculation and undertones would miraculously die a natural death. Molly would then go home. The episode would be forgotten and her good name would remain unblemished because he would announce that they were *married*. A few months down the road there would be a discreet mention in the press that he had obtained a divorce.

Impervious to Azrael's brooding silence, Molly splashed her face in the pool and dried it again on the soggy towel before digging her feet into her shoes. Freshened up, she hurried back to Azrael. He reached for her hand and she shot him a startled look.

'All you do is smile and in minutes we will be leaving,' he assured her bracingly.

'And I'll be going home?' she pressed.

'Within a few days…once we get your passport problem sorted out,' Azrael extended smoothly.

Nothing could have prepared Molly for the sheer melodramatic behaviour of the crowd waiting outside the cave. People fell down on their knees and wailed to the heavens; people wept with relief at the very sight of Azrael and had to be restrained by the soldiers from surging forward and embracing him. She had never seen such a fevered public demonstration of emotional attachment in her life. Throughout cameras flashed, questions were shouted and ignored and commentators stood by talking into microphones. Molly was so taken aback by the extravagant furore that Azrael need not have worried that she might say something inappropriate: shock had completely silenced her.

Silence fell when Azrael spoke in his own language and she saw surprise and other unrecognisable emotions cross faces in rapid succession. Smiles broke out. Heads were dipped. Eyes flew in Molly's direction and lingered and she froze. Whatever Azrael was saying appeared to be welcome news that both soothed and pleased his audience.

'Well, whatever you said went down very well. Everyone seemed to lighten up,' Molly commented as they trudged towards a helicopter, literally surrounded by a phalanx of heavily armed soldiers.

Azrael shot her a warning glance and she heaved a sigh and mimicked a zip being drawn across her lips. Well, Azrael hadn't lightened up any, which was no surprise to her. His conscientious little assistant, Butrus, was talking rapidly and very quietly on his mobile phone, a troubled expression stamped on his face. It seemed that the emergency as such was not yet quite over as far as he was concerned. Molly leapt up into the helicopter and settled in the seat Azrael indicated. He had rescued her, she reminded herself resolutely, so she could be quiet and biddable in public...as long as she could still shout at him in private.

Of course, there wouldn't be much opportunity for that now, she registered. Or any need. After all, she had agreed not to report Tahir to the police, which meant that Azrael had no further need to have any more personal or private meetings with her. She would be stowed in a guestroom until the passport business was sorted out and then conveyed home. Her sojourn in Djalia would soon just be an exotic memory of her brief visit to another world. And it definitely was another world, she acknowledged, staring out at the sweeping golden sand dunes interspersed by craggy rock formations sculpted into weird shapes by the elements. Azrael had called the elements violent and perverse and those words reminded her of the feelings he inspired in her.

It would be *good* to get away from all the emotional and physical turmoil Azrael had unleashed in her, she told herself firmly. She hadn't been sensible, she hadn't been practical, hadn't thought of yesterday or tomorrow or even next week. She had almost had unsafe sex even though she knew that that would be a mistake. Wasn't that a lesson in itself? She had never realised how overwhelming sexual hunger could be. Involuntarily her head turned and found Azrael's bold bronzed profile.

Black stubble outlined his aggressive jawline, highlighting the sculpted perfection of his lips, luxuriant black lashes low over his eyes. Her mouth ran dry and her heartbeat thumped and hurriedly she snatched her gaze away again, mortified by her susceptibility. She was acting like an infatuated teenager, she conceded in exasperation. Yes, it was past time she went home, time to go back to serving drinks with a smile, emptying waste-paper bins and seeking another client who wanted to improve their spoken English. That would all be *real* world enough to set her feet back firmly on the ground.

Azrael strove not to listen to Butrus dealing with an obstreperous member of the Djalian Council, the tribal leaders who acted as Azrael's official advisors and support and, if need be, his critics. And right now the council was shouting up a storm because they wanted a public occasion for his wedding, a day of celebration, a big show. They didn't care how long he had been married, he had to be *seen* to be married. Azrael had not foreseen that outpouring of demands and expectations, but he supposed he should have done and perhaps he would have had he not been so tired. Molly had kept him awake all night and he had not slept the night before that either, troubled as he had been by his conscience. Now his conscience was clear. He had done what he could to protect Molly and now that connection was also almost at an end. He shut his eyes, refusing to think about that.

'A visitor awaits us at the palace,' Butrus whispered as they walked towards the airport building, a spectacular building with a tiled roof that glittered like gold and more chandeliers than a ball room.

Azrael didn't voice his usual objection to the castle being labelled a palace. Butrus believed that a reigning monarch had to live in a palace because it sounded more impressive. Unhappily a Crusader castle briefly occupied during the nineteen twenties and barely updated since scarcely lived up to that grand designation.

'I'm not in the mood for a visitor,' Azrael admitted bluntly. 'Who is he?'

'Our most senior judge, Emir Abdi. He has important information to offer concerning the announcement you made,' Butrus advanced grimly.

Azrael braced himself for an hour of prosy talk

about some esoteric point of law that only a university scholar would find fascinating. Professor Abdi was an erudite man but Azrael was at heart a soldier and a man of action and he found the older man's interminable explanations and arguments trying.

'We are in trouble,' Butrus murmured warningly. 'I did advise you against making that announcement. It has created enormous excitement—'

'It is done and I am always facing trouble of some kind,' Azrael declared resignedly, distracted by the copper glitter of Molly's hair in the sunshine and the very purposeful way she walked. Nothing, not Tahir's infamy, not the worst the desert could throw at her, dimmed Molly's buoyant spirit. She glowed like a light in darkness. What a weird thought to have, he acknowledged with a frown.

Molly was enthralled by the city of Jovan as an SUV carried them down the main thoroughfare. 'It's fantastic,' she told Azrael, staring out at ancient houses, covered markets and elaborate mosques. 'It's so unspoilt—'

'Oh, it's definitely unspoilt,' Azrael agreed wryly. 'Unlike other cities it's been preserved untouched for generations.'

'Tourists would go mad for this. It's so authentic and that's what people want these days,' Molly said enthusiastically, peering out at a little man trying to herd goats out of the traffic onto the pavement, smiling as a much better dressed man went to help him and all the cars stopped.

'People also want hotels and we don't have them,' Azrael said drily.

'So...*build* them!' Molly exclaimed impatiently. 'Embrace a can-do attitude, Azrael. Stop looking at the negatives and concentrate on the positives.'

Butrus listened with appreciation to that practical advice and reflected that his royal employer would have to embrace that attitude sooner than he thought, if Professor Abdi was to be believed and there was no one in Djalia who knew the law better than he.

'I hope I get a little time for sightseeing,' Molly

continued hopefully, shooting Azrael a smile brimming with interest.

'We will see.' Azrael compressed his shapely mouth, refusing to meet those sparkling eyes, seeking distance from the intimacy they had established. He would not be controlled by his libido as he had been in the cave. A faint shudder racked him at that recollection of that ferocious lust and the reality that he could have seduced a virgin. The situation could be much worse, he told himself impatiently.

'The palace,' Butrus announced with discernible pride as the car passed below a stone portcullis.

Azrael's jawline squared because he expected a disparaging comment about the ancient medieval building sprawling in front of them.

'What wonderful gardens!' Molly carolled in astonishment when she glimpsed the lush trees and colourful borders bounding a central fountain. 'My goodness, that must take so much work and watering in this heat.'

'It does indeed,' Butrus responded warmly. 'But

we are very partial to the greenery in gardens and the peace to be found there.'

Molly finally focused on the stone structure before them. 'Your people must be very fond of castles,' she remarked naïvely, thinking of the desert fortress.

'The castles were all built by Djalia's invaders,' Azrael countered deflatingly. 'And the décor and the level of comfort hasn't moved on much since the fourteenth century.'

'But think of the history and the people who must have lived here over the centuries,' Molly enthused, determined not to encourage him in his negative outlook.

The wall of heat that met her when she climbed out of the car daunted her a little. The stone portico over the entrance cooled her and she accompanied the two men into a wide tiled hallway, obviously a more recent addition to the historical structure. A crowd of staff were gathered there, all bowing very low. In fact a couple of the women fell on their knees in front of Molly, and she didn't know what to do and shot Azrael a dismayed glance. He spoke softly and a sensible older woman from the back of the crowd moved forward to receive instructions.

'Haifa oversees the household. She will show you to your room,' Azrael advanced. 'She speaks a little English.'

Molly followed Haifa up a curving turret staircase and then along a stone corridor. She was beginning to realise that the castle was considerably larger than first impressions had suggested and had evidently been much altered and extended over the years. She was shown into a room furnished with faded grandeur and some rather exotic pearl inlaid furniture that included a massive bed hung with regal blue draperies. An adjoining room contained bathroom facilities that were newly installed but unfinished. A shower cabinet sat in pieces in one corner, plumbing equipment filling it but the other facilities appeared intact and functional.

'We bring food,' Haifa assured her, showing her across the corridor to a sitting room that was bare but for a beautiful rug and a low table. 'Please wait, Your Highness.'

Your Highness? Molly's eyes widened. Who did this woman think she was? Or was it simply her lack of English at fault? Maybe the poor woman had assumed she was some visiting royal dignitary. Reluctant to embarrass or confuse Haifa by trying to correct her, Molly folded down on her knees by the table. A mere minute later a procession of servants filed in bearing dishes and enough food to supply a banquet. Without speaking, Molly indicated her choices and received selections and finally sat back to eat, although it was not a very comfortable experience with all the servants stationed by the wall, clearly intent on watching her every move and springing to attend to any request she might have. She ate quickly and returned to her room but even there it wasn't possible to be alone. Haifa arrived with two young smiling women and laid out dress after dress on the bed for her examination. If she liked nothing, more would be forthcoming, Haifa assured her in dumbshow.

Molly quickly picked one of the silk, heavily embroidered dresses to forestall a further parade of fashion options. She was desperately in need of a change of clothes and too well aware of the fact to be choosy. Underwear was brought next in a choice of sizes. It was lingerie from some very fancy provider, each piece beribboned, lacy or embroidered and generally very flimsy, Molly registered, unimpressed. But, keen to replace the bra that had vanished in the cave, she went into the bathroom to try some stuff on and returned with the items that fitted her. Nightwear and summer sandals were produced for her examination then and she had to suppress an impatient sigh while wondering if there was some assumption that she would be staying in Djalia for months without luggage or clothing of her own. Garments accepted and duly admired, she was still not left in peace. Only when one of the women had been allowed to run her a bath was she finally left alone to sink into the warm, rose-scented water and relax.

Azrael, however, had never been further from

relaxation. He was in shock and struggling to hide it while asking all the relevant questions of his very long-winded legal expert.

'Marriage by declaration has been on our statute books for hundreds of years,' Professor Abdi had declared. 'But it has not been used since your great-grandfather ran off with Sheikh Hussein's daughter in the nineteen twenties. He wanted the law retained so that nobody could ever accuse him of not being legally married.'

Azrael had no interest in his rackety great-grandfather's history. All he remembered about him was that he had caused an enormous scandal by kidnapping a woman on the morning of her wedding to another man. That he had married her had been the least of his sins.

'To recap, you're telling me,' Azrael breathed tautly, 'that, even today in Djalia, a man can marry a woman simply by *declaring* that she is his wife?'

'In front of witnesses. The marriage contract is verbal and complete as long as there are witnesses—'

'But what about the bride's consent?' Azrael demanded. 'In such a situation the woman has not given her consent.'

'In law she does not have to give consent for the union to be binding and legal,' the professor assured him. 'You must appreciate that such arrangements were common hundreds of years ago when women were viewed as property.'

'Hundreds of years ago in a different world,' Azrael groaned through gritted teeth.

'Even so, such a marriage is, while unusual, very traditional,' Djalia's most senior judge told him, as if that might constitute good news. 'Naturally, however, everyone expects a more formal ceremony to follow.'

'I will be honest with you, Emir,' Azrael murmured, drawing himself up to his full imposing height. 'I declared that Miss Carlisle was my wife to protect her reputation and, if asked, I intended to say that I had married her in London at the Djalian Embassy last year, which would have been impossible to disprove.'

'Now you need say no such thing or indeed

make any explanations whatsoever,' Emir Abdi told him cheerfully. 'By ancient law, you are now a married man and the young lady is your legal wife. May I wish you both every happiness, Your Majesty—'

'Are you telling me that I would have to get a *divorce* to regain my freedom?' Azrael pressed in disbelief.

'But you are not thinking of divorce,' Butrus broke in to state in haste.

'Hashem made divorce a dirty word within the royal family,' the professor agreed with a censorious frown. 'He had as many brides as that English King in the Tudor times…what was his name?'

'Henry VIII. Our King will not be emulating him,' Butrus asserted confidently.

'An instant divorce would be seen as questionable and it would be unpopular,' the professor opined warily. 'People would be very disappointed, but of course if in *time* you—'

'There will not be an instant divorce,' Azrael swore with determination, registering that his options were few and getting fewer with every word the older man voiced. 'Thank you very much for your advice, Emir, and let us please do whatever it takes to get the law of marriage by declaration *off* the statute books. We must be seen to move with the times.'

Azrael reeled away from that meeting with his usual cool fracturing fast. He was married, legally married, and there was nothing he could do about it because, even if he was desperate enough to admit that he had lied in the first place, the public declaration of marriage he had made would still stand. He breathed in deep and slow, striving for calm.

'That was…enlightening,' he conceded quietly, for want of any better word. 'I must discuss the situation with…with my wife.'

His wife. It changed everything. *His* wife.

'Prince Firuz is eager for you to call him,' his assistant informed him. 'I expect news of your marriage has reached Quarein.'

'That is one phone call that can wait,' Azrael declared without hesitation.

CHAPTER SIX

AZRAEL WANTED A shower and a change of clothes and he headed straight for his bedroom, it not having occurred to him that the staff would have lodged Molly in the same room. He crossed the threshold at the same time as she erupted out of the bathroom accompanied by a cloud of billowing steam. He came to a very sudden halt and stared, for with her spectacular curves enhanced by turquoise silk panties and a matching lace bra, her pink bath-warmed skin gleaming through every tiny aperture of the lingerie, Molly was a vision of stupendous sexiness.

'What are you doing in here?' Molly gasped, racing to the bed to snatch up the dress she had left there and hold it up against her to provide cover.

'This is my room,' Azrael admitted, wishing

she would lower the dress a little to give him another riveting glimpse of the full creamy mounds of her breasts cradled in that low-cut bra. The hardening at his groin was unavoidable. 'I did not realise you were in here.'

'Why was I put in your room?' Molly enquired with a frown, retreating at speed back into the bathroom to get dressed. 'Be out in a minute!' she called, yanking the dress down over her head and forcing her arms into it.

'This is the only bedroom with a private bathroom,' Azrael told her truthfully.

Very much ruffled and still clawing her wet hair out from below the dress, Molly emerged again, acknowledging that it was fortunate that she was not particularly vain because Azrael kept on seeing her at her worst. 'Oh…right—'

'We'll talk after I change. You could wait for me in the room next door. I have ordered coffee for us,' he told her as he rifled through a chest of drawers to pull out items of clothing.

Still in her bare feet and very flushed, Molly left the room and padded along the corridor to a spacious room that contained antique armchairs. A servant arrived with a tray and a plate of tiny sugary delicacies. Molly munched through one while she waited for Azrael and wondered how soon she would be travelling home. What was he planning to do about the passport problem? Contact the British Embassy on her behalf? But then they would naturally want to know how she had contrived to travel to Djalia *without* a passport. Azrael would not want to be forced into an explanation on that issue. Why was everything so difficult? she thought ruefully.

Azrael sent all the staff back to their quarters before he left the bedroom. Sheathed in jeans and a white linen shirt, he joined Molly.

'Coffee?' she asked politely, intending to play hostess and then looking up and fully taking him in and almost gasping at his sheer impact. Azrael was always gorgeous, no matter what he wore. In fitted jeans and a shirt that delineated every line of his lean, powerful body, with his long black hair feathering damply back from his brow, he was breathtakingly handsome.

'Thank you. I can look after myself,' Azrael asserted, pouring a cup of black coffee and heaping several spoonsful of sugar into it.

'You use a lot of sugar,' Molly could not resist remarking.

'Yes. I like it.' The flash of perfect white teeth gleaming in his half-smile made a lecture on dental health seem redundant. 'We have a problem that we must discuss. I want you to take a deep breath if you feel like shouting and listen. Do you think you could do that?'

'I'm not sure,' Molly parried a tinge weakly, still reeling as she was from that utterly alluring smile of his.

'But you can *try*,' Azrael pointed out with emphasis. 'Because shouting will get us nowhere in our current predicament.'

Her smooth brow indented. 'What predicament?'

'First, I will admit that this is all *my* fault,' Azrael intoned gravely. 'I said something on impulse which turned out to be a very bad idea but my intentions were good.'

Molly nodded, wondering what on earth he was talking about.

'When we walked out of the cave I made an announcement. I was unable to be honest about why you were staying with me at the desert fortress as that would have meant exposing Tahir,' he explained. 'I knew that there would be speculation that you were my mistress—'

'Your *mistress*?' Molly stressed in lively astonishment. 'Are you serious?'

'What else would I be doing hidden away at the fortress with a secret female guest?' Azrael fielded drily.

Molly clashed with glittering dark golden eyes and her face suddenly burned hot as fire, forcing her to trail her gaze away again and focus on the ornate coffee pot. Was the desert fortress where Azrael took women? *Of course*, there were women in his life, she told herself impatiently. He was too heart-stoppingly beautiful not to have a constant procession of equally beautiful women in his bed and because Djalia was a conservative place he would naturally have to be discreet about his liaisons.

Azrael breathed in deep. 'I didn't want you to be subjected to that type of unpleasant rumour and targeted by the press. It would have damaged your reputation.'

Molly tilted her head back and studied him in wonderment. 'If I lived in Victorian times, I expect I would have worried about my reputation but not these days—'

'I do not think you—an innocent woman— would have enjoyed the sort of opinions that would have been bandied about in the press,' Azrael asserted. 'And you did not deserve such a humiliating experience after what Tahir had already done to you. When I faced the crowd outside the cave I wanted to protect you from adverse comment of any kind and for that reason I said you were my *wife*.'

A pin-dropping silence fell. Rigid in her chair, Molly stared at him as if he had been telling a joke and she were still waiting to hear the punchline.

Relieved by her lack of reaction, Azrael went on

talking. 'I spent six months in London last year, forging useful alliances while I waited to make the final push of our campaign against Hashem. Few people have any idea what I did during that period and, if asked, I intended to say that I had met and married you while I was living in London—'

Molly's green eyes were huge and her lower lip had dropped. He had so much more imagination than she would ever have dreamt, she registered in awe, but he also had an insanely honourable streak a mile wide. 'What a crazy, crazy thing to have done in your position!' she exclaimed in consternation. 'What on earth got into you?'

'Sadly that is not the end of the story,' Azrael extended grudgingly. 'I have since learned that that simple public statement that we are married is accepted in law in Djalia as a legal declaration of marriage. That is what I have to tell you. According to our most senior judge we are genuinely husband and wife now.'

Very slowly, as if her limbs were stiff, Molly

rose from her seat. 'No…that's not possible,' she told him firmly.

'I wish it were not but that is the situation as it stands,' Azrael countered grimly. 'We are legally married.'

Molly looked at him in disbelief. 'We can't be. You admitted it was your fault and that it was a mad impulse. You said something…foolish, so now you *fix* it.'

Azrael threw his wide shoulders back. 'I'm afraid I can't.'

'Of course you can,' Molly shot back at him half an octave higher in her mounting frustration. 'Of course you can fix it! You told me that *you* were the law in Djalia.'

'If only it *were* that simple, Molly,' Azrael sliced back. 'But it is not. Many other factors are involved here—'

'I don't care about other factors. I only care about me!' Molly snapped back roundly, ringlets dancing round her flushed cheeks. 'You *unfix* this stupid marriage or I'll be guilty of murder!'

'It is unthinkable for me to request an immediate divorce. It would look very bad, as if I am a man who does not know his own mind, a man who casts a woman off without even living with her for a few months—'

'While the real truth is that you're nutty as a fruitcake and locked in the ethics of a bygone age!' Molly threw at him at full volume. 'Who the heck but you would worry about a woman's *reputation* in this day and age?'

'I am not ashamed of an honourable urge to protect you—'

'I don't need protecting!' Molly yelled at him at the top of her voice. 'I'm a strong, independent woman, perfectly capable of looking after myself—'

'But not when you're being kidnapped and not when you're lost in the desert,' Azrael derided.

'And only you would *dare* to throw that at me!'

'It is the truth,' Azrael pointed out without hesitation. 'In the space of a few days I have rescued you twice from dangerous situations. Now I find myself in a position where I need to ask *you* to be understanding and reasonable.'

'You were not reasonable with me!' Molly flung at him straight off, green eyes electric with anger. 'You threatened to keep me a prisoner until I agreed not to slap charges on Tahir, but now I do understand one thing. The Djalian royal family are all crazy as loons. Your brother kidnaps me, you imprison me and tell me we're married without me even being asked how I feel about that—'

'I am sure you feel as trapped and resentful as I do,' Azrael cut in.

Molly lost colour and tossed her head, turning away defensively, wondering why she wasn't warming to that honest admission of his the way that she should. He felt trapped and resentful at the idea of being married to her. When she didn't want to be married to him in the first place, how could that acknowledgement hurt her feelings? Why did she feel very much as though he had just smacked her in the face with a wounding truth?

'We can't possibly be married when I didn't agree to it,' she told him dismissively, taking refuge in a more basic argument.

Azrael breathed in deep. 'In the days when that

law was made women didn't have equal rights and were treated in law much the same as a piece of property.'

'This is not the time to be telling jokes, Azrael,' Molly warned him tartly while throwing back her slim shoulders as if she was trying to make her diminutive stature look more physically impressive.

The movement drew the silk taut across her lush breasts, revealing the crowning peaks of her nipples, and Azrael ached the instant he remembered the succulent taste of those ripe buds. 'I am not joking,' he breathed thickly. 'I wish I was.'

'You have to get us out of this marriage and fast!' Molly spelt out fiercely.

'When my people are already celebrating the fact that I have taken a wife?' Azrael shot back at her rawly. 'How would that look?'

Molly tilted her chin, almost tripping over the coffee table when her eyes encountered the shimmering gold of Azrael's smouldering gaze. 'That's really not my problem.'

'But it is,' Azrael contradicted, concentrating

his attention on her lush full mouth instead, his tension pronounced as he fought his arousal. 'You are my wife and my people will look to you to be a queen. Are they to pay for my mistake? My misguided attempt to protect you?'

An angry flush mottled Molly's fair skin and she turned angrily away from him, fury and conflicting feelings pulling her in different directions. He called his attempt to protect her reputation 'misguided', but she knew that her grandfather would have called it noble and would have applauded him for his desire to shield her. Of course, Maurice was an old-fashioned man, a former soldier, who had grown up convinced that women were the weaker sex in need of a strong man to defend them from the harsh realities of life. Indeed, her grandfather was the only person who had *ever* tried to protect Molly from anything…until Azrael came into her life.

She had always had to fight her own survival battles, only leaning on her grandfather while she was a teenager, and she had been so proud once she knew she could stand on her own feet and had felt even stronger when she could repay Maurice's kindness by fighting to ensure he received the best care possible. In a nutshell it shook her rigid that Azrael would even *try* to protect her. It made her feel foolishly fragile and feminine and decidedly envious of women who could take it for granted that they had someone supportive by their side. She liked that he had been willing to make that effort and come to her rescue, even if he had chosen a rescue boat that seemed to be full of dangerous holes.

Furiously shrugging off such irrelevant thoughts, Molly spun back to him, breasts heaving as she dragged in a steadying breath. 'What do you want from me?'

Mesmerised by the voluptuous shift of rounded flesh below the fabric of her dress, Azrael strode over to the window to focus on something less stimulating. He knew what he wanted from her and just then he knew he had never been further from getting it. 'I want you to stay here for a few months and behave as if you are truly my wife,' he admitted in a harsh undertone. 'Then we would be in a better position to reconsider our situation.'

'But I *can't* stay here!' Molly exclaimed. 'I've got responsibilities back home and I have to work to help cover my grandfather's care bills.'

'You could bring your grandfather out to Djalia,' Azrael informed her.

Startled, Molly shook her head vehemently. 'No, that wouldn't work. Change isn't good for him in his current condition. He needs familiar faces and surroundings or he loses touch with the world altogether because he gets so confused,' she explained. 'Moving him is out of the question. I love him dearly. His comfort and contentment for however long he has left have to come first.'

'Then I pick up the bills for his care and you make regular visits back to London to spend time with him,' Azrael suggested.

Molly bristled. 'You can't just reorganise my entire life to suit you!' she condemned.

'If the reorganisation brings a positive result for many, why not? Is your life in London so much better than it could be here? Is there perhaps…a man involved? Someone you want to return to? I know it was Tahir's belief that you were unattached but who knows whether you told him the truth on that score?' Azrael quipped in a raw undertone.

'Oh, for goodness' sake, I'm totally single!' Molly admitted impatiently. 'I have friends back home but with the three jobs I had I rarely had time to see them. Now at least two of the jobs are gone. Everything that's happened here has screwed up my life and my ability to keep myself, so why the heck can't you just put things back the way they were and fix this problem?'

'You are a very unreasonable woman. You demand the impossible and then look at me accusingly when I fail to deliver.'

'So, *I'm* unreasonable?' Molly pressed a hand to her chest to emphasise that point. 'Nobody's asking you to give up your life and independence!'

'There is nothing I would not sacrifice for my country,' Azrael countered fiercely.

'But you don't own me, so you can't sacrifice me without my consent!' Molly shot back at him tempestuously, green eyes alive with hostility. 'Oh, no, that's right, we are currently standing in the most primitive place on earth where women are as much a man's property as his horse. So maybe you *can* sacrifice me without my consent!'

The very word 'primitive' set Azrael's blood boiling through his veins. He regularly worked eighteen-hour days in his efforts to pull Djalia out of the past and into the future and in that endeavour he had the full support of his people. Hashem had held fast to barbaric practices and laws that had supported his appetite for helpless women and brutality. He had kept a harem of concubines, young females stolen from their families and literally imprisoned. Azrael had been appalled by the stories he had heard after the palace had fallen, but guiltily relieved that Hashem had died of a massive heart attack before he could be put on trial. His country would not have benefitted from a public washing of that amount of dirty laundry.

'Stop…shouting…at…me,' he commanded with lethal quietness.

'I'm a lot more vocal than a horse would be, aren't I?' Molly told him with a certain amount of satisfaction.

'You are my wife and I will treat you with respect,' Azrael breathed tautly. 'But you must treat me with respect too.'

'Not feeling it right now, Azrael…not feeling it at all,' Molly confided, trembling with rage. 'If you marry a woman without her consent, you must roll with the punches when she dares to complain. I am not going to stop shouting because you tell me to!'

Azrael took an almost silent step closer and an ebony brow quirked. 'No?' he queried, golden eyes bright as polished ingots between black framing lashes.

'No!' Molly shouted emphatically back at him.

And Azrael swooped down on her like a hawk, taking her so much by surprise that she yelped in fright as he snatched her off her feet and up into his arms as if she were a lightweight, which she knew she was not.

'Lesson one,' he ground out. 'Do not shout at me when I am tired.'

He kicked open the bedroom door and dropped her down on the bed. 'Lesson two, do not call Djalia primitive or backward—'

As her lips parted furiously to add even less welcome adjectives to the line-up, Azrael laid a hand across her mouth. 'Be quiet,' he told her without hesitation. 'When you insult my country, you offend me. Stop doing it.'

Rigid with rage, Molly jackknifed in an effort to throw him off her because he had her pinned to the mattress by his superior weight. He knelt over her, her arms held still by his hands, and he was much too strong for her to fight.

'I may well be a primitive man because I have had to do many primitive things in my life but I would never treat a woman as a piece of property or physically hurt her. And no, you *know* I am not hurting you at this moment,' he growled, lean, darkly handsome features grim with warning as he made that point.

Molly dragged in a steadying breath. 'I will not insult your country again,' she conceded quietly.

'Thank you...' Azrael freed her arms and sprang off the bed, giving her a fleeting view of his taut behind in denim that roused unfortunate memories of her glimpse of his naked back view in the cave.

Molly's face suffused with burning colour. She watched him lean back against the stone wall by the window like a panther lounging in sunlight. He was so incredibly sexy. Something clenched at her core and she dug her hips into the mattress as if she could squash that feeling, but it filtered up through her in a hot liquid surge, a hungry awareness that refused to die.

'We can work on the shouting. There are ways of learning better control,' Azrael told her helpfully.

'Wanting to slap you won't help me learn better control,' Molly told him.

'You are my wife—'

'Stop it!' Molly reared up against the tumbled pillows. 'Stop saying that!'

'What is the point of arguing with the truth?' Azrael murmured sibilantly, his entire attention welded to her as her glorious hair shimmered in the sunlight like highly polished copper. 'Would you truly strike me in anger?'

Molly shook her shoulders and pursed her lips. 'Probably not. I'm not the violent type, but you do enrage me.'

'I am *trying* to be reasonable,' Azrael confided, scorching dark golden eyes still locked to her.

'Your reasonable isn't like anyone else's reasonable,' Molly framed abstractedly, her veiled gaze resting on his sculpted lips as she relived the taste of them.

'Look on being my wife as a job. I will *pay* you for your compliance,' Azrael spelt out softly. 'I will make it well worth your while to stay here for a few months.'

Molly was mesmerised by his presence and his dark silky voice. He could have been reciting the numeric tables and she would not have reacted. He was offering her the role of wife as a job which paid a salary. That would take care of all her problems at home, she acknowledged reluctantly, but accepting money from him in such circumstances seemed utterly wrong to her.

'I'm not sure,' she muttered in bemusement as Azrael approached the side of the bed and settled down on the edge of it within reach.

'You can trust me,' Azrael intoned. 'I will keep my side of the bargain.'

Her brow furrowed into an anxious frown. 'It's very expensive keeping Maurice in that care home, but I do only pay weekly top-up fees. The authorities cover most of his costs because he had very little money of his own,' she admitted ruefully. 'He's happy at Winterwood. I sold my mother's jewellery to pay the extra charges but I have only enough funds left to cover next month's bill.'

'I will take all that responsibility from your shoulders,' Azrael purred, brushing a stray ringlet back from a delicately flushed cheek to gaze down at her. 'I would be honoured to help you care for your only living relative, but I think it is very sad that you were forced to sell your mother's jewellery to meet the obligation.'

'It was only a ring and a brooch that belonged to my grandmother,' Molly muttered shakily.

The brush of his fingertips across her cheekbone made her want to reach up a hand and touch him back, but she knew, meeting the burning dark gold of his eyes, that what she wanted would only encourage the kind of dangerous intimacy that neither of them should want. There was a burn at the junction of her body, a hot, liquid throb of awareness that made her achingly conscious of a part of her body she had always ignored, and she shifted her hips uneasily. Her breasts were swelling in the cups of her bra, the nipples pushing forward. She sucked in a ragged breath, entrapped by the overwhelming power of what she was feeling.

'I have emeralds the exact colour of your eyes,' Azrael told her huskily, dense black lashes low over his bright eyes. 'You would look magnificent wearing them.'

'Oh, for pity's sake, Azrael...' Molly breathed

helplessly, insanely tempted to reach up and drag him down to her so that her fingers could lace hungrily into his luxuriant black hair. 'I've never worn proper jewellery in my life.'

His hands settled around her waist and he lifted her across him, bringing her down on his lean, powerful thighs. 'Open your mouth for me,' he breathed thickly, one hand curling into her hair to tip her head forcibly back over his arm.

He tugged at her lower lip with the edge of his teeth and a low whimper of sound escaped her. She opened her mouth and he delved deep and she jerked, almost pained by the new sensitivity of her awakened body. He claimed her mouth with a sensual savagery that was as intensely erotic as the hand tracing the silken line of her inner thigh. Instinctively she parted her thighs, craving more, *needing* more.

He traced the taut fabric stretched over her heated core and her heart leapt and her breathing fractured, the craving rising to an unbearable height. He skimmed the edge of her knickers out of his path and gently outlined the tender pink flesh beneath before circling the tight little bud where every nerve ending in her body seemed to reside. Excitement raced through her at a feverish pace, her body shifting restively as he discovered the damp, honeyed slickness between her folds and slid a single finger into her tight opening, gently testing and teasing the entrance at the same time as his thumb rubbed across her. And she cried out, her hips rising to his hand, her body out of her control and rushing for the finish line. The heat and the ache of need combined and she shattered into a sudden intense climax that tore her apart at the seams.

Azrael lowered her limp body back against the pillows and smiled down at her dazed face with satisfaction. 'Instead of arguing, we should go to bed,' he murmured persuasively. 'It would be much more enjoyable.'

'But not very wise,' she whispered giddily. 'We're not going to have a real marriage.'

Azrael said nothing. He knew what he wanted. He would play a waiting game. He would fight for what he wanted. After all, that was nothing new to him. He had always had to fight for everything that was important to him. She wanted him and he could work with that. Their marriage would be real in every way because nothing less would satisfy him.

Initially he had felt trapped and resentful about a marriage that he had not personally chosen. Azrael had always liked to plan major events, but Molly had come at him much like the sandstorm, throwing his life into turmoil, and it was a turmoil that he was discovering he could actually find exhilarating. Molly with her passion, her hot temper and her quick, enquiring mind. Molly, who had no fear of him, no ridiculous reverence and no desire to flatter him. She treated him like an equal and that was a very precious trait to find in a woman, Azrael acknowledged, because all his life he had been treated as different, separated by his royal birth from other men even when he was a soldier in training. He had always been a loner, but with Molly he no longer felt alone. So, why would he want to part with a woman so uniquely perfect to be his wife?

A knock sounded at the door and he frowned, vaulting upright with a weary sigh. If he didn't get some sleep soon he would be a zombie.

'You can fly home to make arrangements in London and pack your possessions up,' he suggested calmly. 'Perhaps you should choose a wedding dress there—'

'A wedding dress?' Molly repeated in astonishment.

'We have to stage a proper wedding to please people.' Azrael opened the door to find Butrus wearing an apologetic expression. 'Yes?'

'Prince Firuz is here in person.'

Azrael's expressive mouth tightened. 'I'll join him downstairs in a few minutes.'

Molly slid uneasily off the bed. 'A *proper* wedding?' she questioned.

'It is expected of us,' Azrael admitted, shedding his shirt to reveal a muscular torso straight out of a centrefold.

Self-conscious, Molly moved over to the window, turning her back on him, listening to the sound of a closet door being opened. 'I'm not sure

I can meet the sort of expectations which will be focused on me. I'm a very ordinary girl.'

'You are extraordinary. Look how you've looked after your grandfather, look how you've dealt with everything that's happened here. True, there was a little shouting, but you have great heart and tremendous courage and compassion,' Azrael countered with ringing conviction.

Molly smiled, whirling round to look at him to discover he was back in formal apparel, his hair covered, a pristine long white buttoned tunic teamed with a gold-braided cloak. 'I'll have a go at being your wife,' she murmured. 'But that's the most I can promise.'

Dark golden eyes gleamed over her smiling face. 'That you agree to try is enough.'

CHAPTER SEVEN

'I JUST CAN'T believe you're married,' her friend Jan carolled, shaking her dark braided head as she cradled her newborn son, Robbie, on her lap. 'Tell me *everything.*'

A week had passed since Molly had flown out of Djalia, travelling on a Djalian diplomatic passport. It had been a crazy busy week. She had settled her final bills, packed up her sparse possessions and had spent hours every day sitting with her grandfather, who sadly hadn't once recognised her as family but had continually talked about how much her face reminded him of someone. In between times she had shopped and spent more money than she ever had for herself before, utilising the string of credit cards Azrael had given her before her departure. She had bought a summer wardrobe more suitable for Djalia's climate as well as a wedding outfit.

'I mean, the minute I read about you marrying him in the paper, I knew you must have met him while you were giving English lessons at that foreign embassy, but I can't believe you never said anything to me… I saw you two months ago and you never once mentioned him!' Jan complained. 'You also never mentioned that you were planning a trip to his country.'

'That opportunity came up unexpectedly,' Molly admitted wryly.

'I suppose you weren't sure he was thinking of marriage and didn't want to say anything in case nothing came of it. He's a very good-looking guy,' Jan proclaimed enviously. 'I'm not surprised that you kept him to yourself—'

'It all happened very fast,' Molly interposed. 'I'm not sure I can believe it's really happening… the wedding, I mean.'

'I think those three bodyguards waiting for you in my hall say it's happening all right.' Jan laughed. 'Clearly, Azrael either wants to ensure that you're safe everywhere you go or that you don't run away! I hope you appreciate that I didn't say a word to the journalists when I was approached. You only worked for my cleaning firm part-time but I didn't see that was anyone's business but yours, and when I was asked about your family background I said they had all passed away before I even met you.'

'Thanks but you needn't have worried,' Molly replied ruefully. 'It's this wretched hair. Someone recognised me from the photographs that were taken at the airport and phoned up the newspaper to say that I was a cleaner on the night shift where they worked. I wasn't prepared for the cameras the day I arrived home and I looked such a mess—'

'No, you didn't. You simply looked surprised that anyone would bother taking a picture of you!' Jan giggled. 'But, Molly, you're going to be a queen…of course the press is interested in who you are and where you came from.'

'Let's hope they don't dig up any of my step-mother's relatives or I'll be christened a wild devil child,' Molly groaned, grateful for the reality that the bodyguards Azrael had insisted travel with her kept the press at a safe distance.

'It's the Cinderella story, the rags-to-riches dream that draws them,' Jan commented, shaking her head. 'But I'm not sure I could face living in a foreign country for the rest of my days and, by all accounts, Djalia is a pretty backward place—'

'No, it's a country on the brink of transformation,' Molly corrected without hesitation.

'The women I saw in photographs were wearing *ankle*-length dresses,' Jan protested in an aghast tone of voice.

'Only because the former dictator imposed a modest dress code on women. Now the female population simply need access to shops to buy modern clothes. There's a lot of work to be done in opening up the retail trade,' Molly told her.

'You sound like a politician,' Jan whispered in dismay.

'No, it's not that. Azrael asked one of the diplomats to make up prompt sheets for me on the sort of facts I should know about Djalia and I've been memorising them and now my head is buzzing with all this random information,' Molly confided ruefully.

'He gives you *prompt sheets* the week before your wedding? Who is this guy?'

'He was only trying to help me,' Molly parried, registering in surprise that she had become very protective of Azrael. 'If I get asked questions, I don't want to talk nonsense now that I'm supposed to be representing Djalia with him.'

And it was true. Molly was feeling the pressure that she had not appreciated would go with the role she had accepted because she didn't want to stumble and embarrass Azrael by saying or doing the wrong thing. It was the kind of responsibility she had never had before, the kind of responsibility she had belatedly realised that Azrael carried daily during the three days she had stayed at the palace before leaving for London.

He had not returned to the bedroom she had slept in, even though it was supposedly *his* bedroom. Butrus had casually let drop that Azrael often worked late into the night and slept on the couch in his office and that Prince Firuz, Tahir's father, had kept Azrael up talking until the early hours that first night. Regardless, Molly had barely seen Azrael except at mealtimes while he racked up office hours dealing with his duties. She had slept alone, which she had told herself was a good thing. Sex would muddy the waters of their relationship, making it personal when it was supposed to be a practical arrangement to get Azrael out of a tight corner. In addition he was *paying* her for her services and she could hardly sleep with a man in that scenario and either still respect herself or feel that their relationship could have a future.

No, Molly believed that she was much more worldly wise than that and she was determined to protect herself from getting her heart broken. Beautiful Azrael was not going to settle for an ordinary woman, who had once cleaned and served drinks, as a wife. He had admitted that he felt trapped and resentful and when he felt the time was right and the bridal fuss was only a mem-

ory he would move on from her without a backward glance.

Looking a little awkward, Jan passed her a Sun-
day newspaper supplement. 'I wondered if you'd
seen this so I kept it for you…there's an article
about Azrael and Djalia.'

'No, I hadn't seen it. I'll read it when I get back
to the hotel,' Molly said, tucking it into her new
capacious leather bag with enthusiasm.

'It's not very nice…the article, I mean,' her
friend admitted uncomfortably. 'Please don't be
annoyed with me for giving it to you.'

'Of course not.' But Jan's warning ensured that
Molly had the magazine open even before the
limousine carrying her set off back to the hotel.

The horrid photograph of her arriving back
from Djalia featured and she groaned out loud.
Her hair was frizzy because she hadn't had condi-
tioner when she'd washed it in Djalia. She wore no
make-up because she hadn't had any with her and
the jeans and sweater she had travelled out there
wearing were plain and serviceable rather than
elegant. Frowning at that unflattering photo, she

took a moment or two to appreciate that there was a photo of another woman alongside her own...a sort of comparison set-up, she registered in consternation. And, worst of all, the photo showed Azrael in profile *with* the glossy brunette.

The brunette was Princess Nasira of Quarein, the niece of Prince Firuz and the young woman whom Azrael had reportedly been *expected* to marry. Nasira had gorgeous almond-shaped eyes and elegant black hair in an up-do that glittered with diamond pins. Not only was she a beauty but she also had a degree in politics from the Sorbonne in Paris, spoke half a dozen languages and ran a children's charity in Quarein. The contrast between Molly and Nasira and her many accomplishments, not to mention the Princess's impeccable pedigree, could not have been more painful or obvious, the slant of the article suggesting that Azrael's choice of a British bride was both controversial and surprising. Molly turned pale and chewed her lower lip, wondering why Azrael had never mentioned Nasira to her. He had asked Molly if she had anyone in her life! Why hadn't it occurred to her to ask *him* the same question?

For pity's sake, was that why Prince Firuz had visited the palace that very first evening? Had he arrived on behalf of his niece to demand an explanation from Azrael regarding his sudden acquisition of a foreign bride? Was that why Azrael had slept apart from her? Molly reddened, admitting that she was in conflict when it came to that issue. She had sat up waiting for Azrael to reappear that night and then had lain awake for hours mentally listing all the reasons why she should *not* have sex with him.

In fact she had been all worked up to give him those reasons when he finally reappeared but he had proved a no-show that night and for the two nights that had followed. She never had got to make the speech she had prepared and, although he had phoned her to chat every evening since she had left, it wasn't really the sort of conversation she wanted to stage on the phone…was it?

On the same day as Molly struggled with her wildly see-sawing emotions and urges, Azrael was, most ironically, having a similarly disturbing experience. The British press had done an in-depth investigation into his bride's modest background, which had provided an unpleasant surprise.

In the wake of all Molly had said concerning her ailing grandfather in his care home, Azrael had been extremely surprised to read that Molly's maternal grandfather had *died* long before she was born and her paternal grandfather almost as long ago. He had instructed Butrus to carry out the same research and, to Azrael's dismay, Butrus had confirmed the information.

Molly did *not* have a living grandfather, which could surely only mean that she had lied to Azrael. He had put a comparatively small amount of money in her bank account to enable her to make initial payment arrangements with the care home she had mentioned. But if the grandfather didn't exist, he could only assume that Molly had quite deliberately told him a sob story, intended to play on his sympathies. And the sob story had worked a treat, Azrael reflected grimly. He *had* been impressed that she was willing to make sacrifices to assist in the care of an elderly relative and he had not been suspicious when she'd insisted that *she* deal with the care home personally rather than allowing Azrael's staff to contact the facility on her behalf.

Exactly when had he become so naïve and trusting? Azrael asked himself angrily. His sexual liaisons with women had taught him that his wealth did, if anything, matter more to those women than his looks or character and that the more expensive his gifts, the more they liked him and sought to please. That financial slant had turned him off, making him feel as if he was, in some sleazy way, paying for sex.

Essentially, Molly was no different from those avaricious women, he registered with innate revulsion. She was obviously determined to enrich herself as much as possible from their marriage and the story about the non-existent grandfather and the care home had merely been utilised to impress him and give her a means to demand the money she wanted. Absurdly, from his point of view it was a derisory amount of money, he acknowledged ruefully, but possibly, having come from a less privileged background, it seemed like a *lot* of money to Molly. Even so, it wasn't the amount, it was the means she had employed to get that money. He was disappointed in her, furious that she had put together so elaborate a lie and more disturbed by the lying, the greed and the calculation involved than the actual cash.

Why had he expected her to be perfect? No man and no woman was perfect, he told himself logically. She had fooled him, however, and the bitter sense of disgust lingered with him, no matter how hard he tried to shake it off. How the hell could he stay married to a woman with such low principles? And yet, he really did not have a choice on that score…

Early evening, Molly returned to the building which Butrus studiously referred to as a palace and Azrael called a castle. She grinned at the recollection, recognising that Azrael was blunt in his opinions in comparison to the older man and liking that trait in him. He hadn't phoned her before her departure from London and she had wondered why, and had even been a little disappointed not to hear his voice, but she had simply assumed that he was too busy to call her. Having taken pains with her appearance, Molly realised that she was quite ridiculously eager to see Azrael again and she scolded herself for feeling what she *knew* she should not feel. But nothing could slow the fast beat of her heart or the butterflies penned up in her stomach as, with a warm smile at the staff waiting to greet her, she hurried on and sped upstairs to what she now knew to be the private royal wing of the castle.

'Where's Azrael?' she asked Butrus breathlessly after her whirlwind search of those rooms failed to reveal a keen bridegroom awaiting the woman due to become his bride the following day.

His benevolent face somewhat stiff, Butrus forced a smile. 'The King is in his office, Your Majesty.'

'Molly will do, Butrus,' she said comfortably. 'We don't need to be formal behind closed doors.'

Butrus nodded while Molly smoothed damp palms down over the fitted green dress she had purchased in a high street store. The dress might have cost more money than Molly had ever spent on one item before and the shoes almost as much but she had an almost overwhelming need to look her very best at her next meeting with Azrael. After all, he had first seen her unconscious and he had never seen her either wearing make-up or dressed up. If it was possible, and she was mortified by her own vanity, she wanted to blow him away...

Azrael glanced up from his laptop when Molly walked into his office without even knocking. He would make her knock in future, he thought sternly, dark as night eyes flaring gold as he took in her altered appearance. She looked spectacular, her shapely figure and terrific legs delineated in a figure-hugging dress and high heels. He went rigid as he connected with bright green eyes full of warmth and vivacity and the smile on that luscious pink mouth. Sexual hunger flooded him with such intensity, he snatched in a fracturing breath, battling the desire that his gold-edged cloak would conceal to stand up.

Molly's face lit up the instant she saw him, the excitement she couldn't control flying up inside her like fireworks shooting across the heavens. He should have seemed so foreign to her in his traditional clothing, she told herself weakly, but when she laid eyes on his lean, darkly beautiful face, he was simply Azrael and nothing could detract from the surge of heat and happiness travelling through her. Yet this same man had not even come to welcome his bride back to Djalia, her brain reminded her stubbornly, and she struggled to control her fiery emotions.

'I can see that you're busy as usual,' she said lightly, recognising his Mr Grumpy expression for what it was. 'But you should have at least come to say hello.'

'Should I have?' Azrael countered in a steely tone she had not heard from him before because he was determined to confront her with her dishonesty.

'Yes, you should've done,' Molly responded

simply. 'It was sort of a little disrespectful that you didn't make the effort and I'm sure it looked strange to the staff—'

'My staff do not judge me and I am not disrespectful,' Azrael parried with hauteur.

'Obviously you're not in the best mood,' Molly remarked frankly, fully registering that reality from his rigid stance and forbidding expression. 'And I'm not very good with moody people. I was taught that it's bad manners to take your moods out on other people.'

'As was I,' Azrael gritted, fighting a very strong urge to grip her by the shoulders and demand to know how she could smile and act hurt when she had been lying to him almost from the moment he had met her.

'Clearly it didn't work in your case,' Molly muttered hesitantly, reluctant to have a row with him the night before the wedding and deciding that sometimes the best policy was to retreat rather than to fan the flames. 'Look, I'll go back upstairs, leave you to work in peace—'

Azrael settled sizzling dark golden eyes on her

troubled face. 'You *lied* to me!' he accused with staggering abruptness, unable to restrain his fury any longer.

Hugely taken aback by the accusation and with her hand already on the door knob, Molly frowned. 'I've never lied to you about anything—'

'I have found you out. There *is* no grandfather in a care home!' Azrael ground out in condemnation. 'He doesn't exist...you made him up!'

Molly was in shock, her lashes fluttering up and down on his lean, darkly angry face as she wondered wildly if he had been drinking, or if indeed there was a whole other crazy side to Azrael that she was only now seeing. She had never seen him that angry and it was more than a little unnerving, she was willing to admit. A very strong sense of self-preservation made her flip open the door and head straight back to the stairs.

'Come back here!' Azrael called after her.

Azrael was *shouting* where he could be heard, Molly registered in disbelief. Azrael, who was very courteous, well-disciplined and always conscious of listening ears. It freaked Molly out.

Thoroughly disconcerted by his uncharacteristic behaviour, Molly fled up the stairs as though all the hounds of hell were on her tail. What did he mean that her grandfather didn't exist? How could he make such an insane allegation?

'I will bring coffee to the salon, Your Majesty,' Haifa assured her at the top of the stairs.

'Not now, thank you,' Molly muttered, nervously conscious that Azrael was thundering up the stairs behind her and hastening on down the corridor.

Behind her she heard him rap out a staccato instruction to the housekeeper and she kept on moving, finally darting into the reception room at the foot of the corridor that opened out onto a charming rooftop garden. The French windows stood wide on the sunlight and, mindful of Azrael's mood, Molly hastily slammed them shut.

'You will explain yourself right now!' Azrael launched at her wrathfully, lodging in the doorway like an immovable rock.

Molly flipped round, her slight body whip taut with tension. The unvarnished anger he could not

hide disturbed her because she could not understand what could possibly have changed between
them while they had been apart. 'How can I explain myself when I don't understand what you're
talking about?'

'Of course you know what I'm talking about!'
Azrael thundered back at her with conviction.

'Do I?' Molly's own temper was finally beginning to rouse in the face of his seething animosity. And the shock of such a welcome when she
had naïvely hoped for a much warmer reception
was affecting her outlook as well. She was learning that she didn't know Azrael as well as she
had fondly believed and she wasn't enjoying what
she was discovering. She was even reconsider-
ing what she had read about Princess Nasira and
wondering just how much she could trust Azrael.
That was a serious question that went right to the
heart of their relationship.

'Do I have to spell out what you have done in
words of a single syllable?' Azrael demanded.

'Yes,' Molly traded sharply. 'How could you

possibly say that my grandfather doesn't exist when I visited him every day I was in London?'

'Your background was exhaustively researched by the British press and I read the article,' Azrael informed her. 'Certain facts about your family tree emerged. You don't have a living grandfather—'

'Maurice may be a little confused but I can assure you that he is very much alive and kicking!' Molly slammed back at him in bemusement.

'Both your grandfathers are dead, the first before you were born, the second when you were a child,' Azrael enumerated grimly. 'So, you lied to me!'

'No, I didn't… I have *never* lied to you!' Molly flung back at him full volume as the first glimmerings of his misapprehension began to connect the dots for her. 'And to accuse me of making up a story that I had a grandfather in a care home… I mean, why on earth would I do that?'

'To engage my sympathies as a means of extracting money from me!' Azrael gritted in disgust. 'You should be ashamed—'

'No, *you* should be ashamed of your nasty, suspicious mind!' Molly shouted back at him furiously. 'I don't need or want your wretched money and I didn't ask you for any of it either! How dare you accuse me of being a lying gold-digger?'

'Those are your words,' Azrael deflected, calming now that he had vented his angry disillusionment but decidedly confused by her reaction. 'Not mine.'

Molly dealt him a look of supreme scorn. 'I can read between the lines, Azrael. I'm not stupid and if this is what you really think of me, it makes me wonder what else you have hidden from me—'

'I have hidden nothing from you—'

'One word.' Molly tossed her coppery head back, ringlets streaming back from her hotly flushed face.

'What word?' Azrael queried, feeling increasingly lost in the dialogue and unable to understand how that had happened when he was in the right and she was in the wrong.

'Nasira,' Molly framed with dark satisfaction.

'Now, are you planning to continue blocking the doorway? Or may I leave the room, Your Majesty?'

Azrael frowned. 'What has Nasira to do with us?'

It wasn't the guilty reaction Molly had been looking for, indeed even expecting after the argument they had had. 'You have secrets too,' she condemned.

'Not about her,' Azrael breathed in bewilderment. 'Only about things you wouldn't want to know about—'

Molly planted a small hand directly in the centre of his hard muscular chest. 'Move!' she told him.

'Why? Where are you going?'

'That's none of your business—'

'Everything you do is my business...you're my wife,' Azrael reminded her without hesitation.

'You have so much to learn about women,' Molly responded with saccharine sweetness as she yanked his lean, powerful body out of her path and slid behind him to stalk back to the bedroom. 'But you won't be learning it from me—'

'What's that supposed to mean?' Azrael demanded rawly, striding after her, dark golden eyes flaming with frustration even as the sway of her curvaceous hips in that dress attracted his grudging attention.

'That when you label a woman a lying gold-digger, she's not going to be your business *or* your wife any more!' Molly completed. 'I've had it up to my throat with Djalia and its freaky King—'

'I am not freaky,' Azrael enunciated with perfect diction.

'But you're not the sharpest tool in the box either,' Molly hazarded with a downright unpleasant glance in his direction. 'Your own Djalian bodyguards have accompanied me to the care home every day to visit my non-existent grandfather. Did you think of checking with them *before* you unleashed all this drama on me? No, you did *not* think.'

And Azrael was confounded by that statement because he knew it was true. He prided himself on his calm control and logic but both had inexplicably gone missing when he most needed them at his disposal. The belief that Molly had lied to him, made a fool of him and deceived him had eaten him alive and his rarely released temper had taken hold of him. For the first time it occurred to him that he might somehow have got it wrong because Molly was not behaving like a guilty person.

'So, explain to me how your grandfather is dead and yet *not* dead,' Azrael demanded quite seriously and with his usual imperious edge.

'It's not happening. I'm out of here, bag and baggage,' Molly told him roundly, grabbing up a suitcase and thinking better of it. 'No, that doesn't belong to me. None of it does. The clothes in these cases were bought with *your* money so they are not mine—'

'Stop this…*now*!' Azrael thundered at her. 'You are not leaving me—'

Glittering green eyes struck his. 'Watch me,' she invited, sashaying out of the door again, carrying only her handbag.

'You're my wife—'

'And you called *me* a lying gold-digger. I will not stay married to a man who thinks that of me!' Molly spat back at him in rage.

'If I have made a mistake I will make up for it,' Azrael swore with touching faith in his own powers of persuasion. 'But you are not leaving me—'

'I am leaving you,' Molly repeated with emphasis. 'And you're not allowed to make mistakes of that magnitude and be forgiven for them! There is no get-out-of-jail-free card here!'

'I will not allow you to leave me,' Azrael shot back at her with suppressed savagery, wondering why she was referring to a prison. 'That option isn't on the table. You are already my wife—'

'Without my consent...*remember*?' Molly reminded him doggedly.

Azrael voiced a very rude English word and snatched her off her feet. 'I don't care. You are not leaving me,' he repeated stubbornly, ignoring her struggles as he carted her back into their bedroom and planted her down on the bed like a rock being settled firmly back into sand. 'This is your home now.'

'You can't force me to stay here against my will and you know you can't!' Molly told him defiantly. 'I'd scream the place down, I'd run away, I'd be a nightmare!'

'Explain your "not dead" grandfather,' Azrael persisted, lounging back against the door to prevent her from trying to leave again.

Molly dealt him a hostile appraisal. 'Why should I?'

'It would be the adult approach.'

'You're one to talk,' Molly snapped. 'You jumped straight to nasty conclusions.'

'My past experiences with women have made me distrustful and cynical.'

Molly closed her eyes tight, furious at the idea of him ever having been with anyone else. It was a totally unreasonable reaction but that was how she felt: as if he was *hers*, body and soul. Such a possessive feeling was not something to celebrate just at that moment, she reflected with self-loathing.

'Explain,' Azrael demanded.

'My grandmother, a widow, married Maurice Devlin when my mother was a baby. My mother's birth father died before *she* was born, never mind my birth. Maurice has always been my grandfather and I rarely remember that we're not related by blood,' she confided truthfully. 'He raised my mother as his daughter. When she died he continued to treat me as his grandchild and I've always thought of him as family…the only family I have.'

'Thank you. That has clarified the situation,' Azrael responded with dignity, torn between relief that his worst imaginings were groundless and anger that he, who prided himself on his cool head and judgement, could have put himself so much in the wrong.

Molly recognised the conflicting emotions chasing across his lean, darkly handsome face and noted the colour rising to accentuate his exotic cheekbones as he accepted the truth of her explanation. She wondered dimly what kind of behaviour his past experiences with women had entailed and crushed a curiosity that she knew would only upset her.

'I am very sorry for my misapprehension,' Azrael murmured gruffly. 'I insulted you.'

He was defensive, wearing his Mr Grumpy expression again and, even aware that she was the injured party, Molly was impressed that he could rise above his pride to apologise. 'I'm still annoyed with you,' she admitted.

Azrael jerked his chin in acknowledgement and studied her with dark intense eyes. 'I lost my temper—'

'We all do from time to time,' she parried, fighting an overpowering desire to wrap her arms round his lean, powerful figure and despising herself for it. 'But I can't overlook the speed with which you chose to believe the worst of me… that's a dangerous level of distrust.'

A very faint spur of panic urged Azrael forward. There was so much he felt that he should be saying but he wasn't used to saying such things and he didn't have the words to explain that she brought something into his life he knew he could not bear to lose. He sank down on the side of the bed and used a long-fingered brown hand to cradle her cheekbone, his thumb tracing the edge of her full, sultry mouth.

'I love the dress,' he said so inanely that he winced for himself but the soft, warm touch of her skin made concentration impossible. 'It looks amazing on you.'

Molly snatched in a startled breath, battling to retain her distance, but the glide of his thumb made her mouth tingle and the compliment could only please.

'The next time you go to London I will accompany you and we will visit your grandfather together,' Azrael declared.

Soothed by that statement of intent, Molly came up on her knees on the bed, drawn by his proximity, mesmerised by the black-lashed drama of his dark golden eyes. 'I'm still furious with you—' she warned him tartly even while her breath fractured in her throat as the familiar scent of him, husky male spiced with an extra degree of exotic, engulfed her.

'Of course.' Azrael bent his head and went for the soft pink lure of her ripe lips, the need to connect with her overwhelming every other rational response.

CHAPTER EIGHT

AZRAEL'S MOUTH ENGULFED Molly's and all the reasons why she shouldn't allow that, including the prepared speech about why intimacy was a very bad idea, simply melted out of her mind as though they had never existed.

He was incredibly good at kissing, she thought vaguely, or maybe it was because she was utterly desperate to be kissed. She didn't know which and she didn't know if it even mattered because Azrael's mouth on hers was pure sensual intoxication. She trailed off his *kaffiyah* to get her hands into his luxuriant black hair and he was very much on board with that approach because he shed his cloak and began to unbutton his tunic while pressing her back against the pillows to savour her lips and let his tongue dance and curl with hers. Sensation awakened there first where with every moist sweep of his tongue her body ratcheted up in tension a little more. Her spine strained to ease the tingling of her nipples and the swelling of her breasts while heat gathered at her feminine core.

Azrael ran the zip down on the dress and then it got complicated because, when he tried to ease the sleeves down to free her arms, the fabric merely stretched and then sprang back into position. With a strangled laugh of amusement, Molly pushed him back and sat up to wrench the clinging dress down over her arms and let it drop to her waist.

'That was a challenge,' Azrael acknowledged, dark golden eyes alive with the same amusement. 'I'm not making a very polished impression here, am I?'

Molly's hands framed his lean dark face and that smile tore the breath from her lungs and melted her somewhere deep down inside. 'You don't need to be…polished with me,' she muttered truthfully.

He gazed down at her as she pushed his black

hair back from his cheekbones, his captured attention sliding down over her reddened mouth to the smooth, freckled slope of her full, round breasts encased in blue and white polka dots, and his broad chest swelled as he dragged in a sustaining breath, enthralled by the vision she made.

'I love your breasts,' he said thickly, sliding his hands beneath her to release the clasp with a dexterity that he was secretly very pleased with.

And then there she was, all creamy glorious perfection, bountiful and soft and firm at the same time. He rubbed a straining pink nipple, his breath laboured as though he had run up a hill as he kneaded and cupped the plump mounds.

'You're truly beautiful,' he told her huskily.

And for the first time in her life, Molly felt as though she was. Of course it certainly helped to have Azrael looking down at her with a kind of wondering pleasure, as if she were a goddess rather than an ordinary woman. The heat coiled between her thighs ramped up another notch, her nipples tightening into distended buds. He captured one between his lips, laved it with his tongue, let his teeth graze the straining peak and a soundless moan of pleasure escaped her and her spine arched.

'Take your tunic off,' she whispered shakily.

He leant back from her and yanked it over his head, too impatient to bother with the remaining buttons, and she had a perfect view of his even more perfect torso. He was all hard, sleek muscle from his wide brown shoulders down to the defined V that ran from his narrow waist down into his pelvis. Muscles from his biceps to his chest to his flat, tight stomach rippled with his every move. In a sudden movement, impatient with the constrictions of his clothing, Azrael sprang off the bed and dropped the tunic before skimming off the loose linen trousers and briefs he wore below.

And there he all was, sooner than she had expected to see him, and her breath caught in her throat at her first glimpse of his arousal. He bent over her, dragging off the stretchy dress, flipping off her shoes, reaching for the band of her knickers.

'No, you're going too fast for me,' Molly warned him, her face tomato red. 'Slow down. I haven't done this before…remember?'

'You can't fault me for enthusiasm, *aziz*,' Azrael said playfully. 'But I will slow down.'

'Thank you,' she said unevenly, taking the opportunity to push back the bedding and slide beneath the concealing cover of the sheet. 'I'm sorry I'm a bit shy…but I don't think you have a shy bone in your body.'

'Never thought about it,' Azrael admitted. 'I would've been punished for being timid or impolite or not doing what it was my obligation to do—'

'Punished?' Taken aback, Molly leant over him to stare down at him. 'Who would've punished you?'

'Firuz was a very strict stepfather. I was beaten a lot,' Azrael confided with the calm of someone who appeared to accept that such a childcare approach was perfectly normal.

'But that's dreadful,' Molly exclaimed in horror.

'I survived. I can survive any mistreatment,'

Azrael countered with pride. 'I was brought up to be tough.'

'Would you treat your own children—?'

'No, of course not!' Azrael studied her with incredulity. 'Firuz is a tyrant in his own household. I withstood his punishments for my mother's sake. She would've suffered if I had defied him or rebelled. *My* children will never be beaten,' he swore vehemently.

Molly's eyes stung and she pressed a helpless kiss to a bare brown shoulder. 'You had the most horrendous childhood.'

'It is the past,' Azrael reminded her gently. 'I do not look back.'

'I suppose that's one way of dealing with it,' Molly mumbled.

'It is my duty to be strong,' Azrael pointed out, glittering dark eyes roaming over her troubled face. 'Why does that upset you?'

'Oh, no reason,' Molly hastened to assure him chokily.

A seeking hand smoothed up over a curved hip and settled on a lush pink-tipped breast. 'You have too much heart, *aziz*,' he intoned huskily, sliding half over her to plunge his mouth hungrily down on hers.

And serious thought along with that conversation vanished then, lost in the rising tide of her physical responses. He sucked the tips of her breasts, contrived to dispose of her last garment without her noticing and smoothed a skilled hand up to the junction of her thighs where she throbbed and pulsed with a fierce craving for more that she barely understood. Azrael shifted down over her, lithe as a jaguar, his skin pure bronze against the white sheet, and his black hair brushed her thigh.

She had never wanted and had never felt anything like the delicious physical torment that followed. Her fingertips raked the sheet and then plunged into his thick hair. She cried out, teeth gritting, spine arching as the sweet agonising sensations grew in intensity until her lower body was taut with the hot, churning tightness of inner need and hunger. Her body writhed convulsively as she soared to her peak, unleashed waves of pleasure roaring through her in a glorious shot of relief and delight.

'Tell me if I hurt you,' Azrael told her hoarsely, rising over her, pushing her thighs back when she was already weak and boneless with satiation.

She felt the push as his bold shaft entered her, eyes widening at the unfamiliar sensation. Her body was primed for him and he groaned with unashamed pleasure over her and the glittering golden satisfaction in his stunning eyes excited her more. His lean hips shifted fluidly between her thighs as he thrust deeper and a sudden sharp little pain made her bite back a cry of discomfort. She hadn't expected her first taste of intimacy to be an entirely pain-free process and she was determined not to spoil it for either of them as he stretched her with his powerful girth.

Azrael growled with uninhibited pleasure, luxuriating in the tight wet welcome of her body. Raging impatient need roared through his long, powerful body but he needed to make it the best it could be for her. Rigid with control, he raised himself to glide in and out of her, filling her up with slowly building speed and intensity.

Molly's head fell back, her eyes shutting as she fought to contain the wild sensations eddying out from the heated ache and tightness in her pelvis. She could feel the hunger climbing again, rising sharply as he ground down on her and then sank harder and deeper, all grace, all power and impossibly erotic. She panted for breath, flying high on the surge of excitement he had incited, the feverish pound of his possession uniting with her racing heartbeat and suddenly she was there again on the heights, her body out of control as her world exploded into white-hot ecstasy. His magnificent body shuddered as he too reached the same completion.

Afterwards, cradled in Azrael's arms, Molly felt as though she was floating in the most sublime contentment she had ever known.

'That was amazing… I want to keep you,' Azrael husked without the smallest warning.

'What?' she mumbled uncertainly.

'I don't want to reconsider our marriage in a

few months' time… I want to keep you,' Azrael reiterated calmly as though that were the simplest sentiment in the world to express.

I want to keep you. Very much as if she were a pet or a piece of property, Molly interpreted in astonishment. 'We didn't discuss anything like that,' she reminded him hesitantly.

'There is nothing to discuss,' Azrael declared, sitting up, so devastatingly handsome in that instant that he literally stole the breath from her straining lungs. 'We both got so carried away we didn't even think of using protection.'

Her eyes flew even wider and she too sat up, clutching at the sheet. 'Protection?' she repeated blankly.

'I forgot,' he told her truthfully. 'I'm sorry—'

'It wasn't safe. A few weeks ago it would've been,' Molly told him worriedly. 'But I missed some pills after Tahir took me because I didn't have them with me here. I was planning to start taking them again at the end of the month.'

'You could be pregnant now, *aziz*,' Azrael declared quietly. 'I was out of my mind with excitement. I did not have control and neither did you but if you *do* conceive—'

'But I don't want to be pregnant!' Molly protested, marvelling that within minutes of feeling closer to him than she had ever felt to any living being, she could then be blindsided by the reality that he thought and functioned on an entirely different plane. 'It's too soon. I'm not ready for motherhood yet.'

Azrael was starting to frown as he slid fluidly off the bed. 'Why the fuss? You're my wife! What could be more natural than to have my child?'

Molly looked heavenward. 'It doesn't work that way in the West. Having children is something a man and a woman discuss and decide on *together*.'

Azrael had tensed, dark eyes flaring with gold lights. 'If choosing *not* to have my child is that important to you, you should have considered the risk for yourself. I forgot but so did you.'

Molly gritted her teeth at a truth she was not in the mood to hear at that moment. Unhappily she wasn't accustomed to having to consider risks in the pregnancy stakes because he was her first lover. Azrael was affronted, as if even the chance to have his child was a wonderful opportunity that no normal woman would wish to evade. Offence was stamped into the grim lines of his lean dark face and the aggressive angle of his stubbled jawline.

Azrael was very much taken aback by Molly's attitude to the risk they had run together. Only as he registered that he had forgotten to use a condom had it occurred to him that he would very much like to have a child with Molly. After all, the only surviving member of his family was his kid brother and his heart warmed at the prospect of having a proper family in the future with children he could call his own.

Ironically he had imagined how warm and loving Molly would be with a child. His own mother had been too distant and reserved to act like the loving, caring mother he had longed to have as a little boy. His instantaneous, idealistic vision of building a happy family with Molly had shattered beneath a withering rejection, which he saw as unfeeling. After all, if she did conceive would she then reject his child or think less of that child because she had not planned its birth? Or were her reservations more basic? Was it simply *his* child she did not want?

'In future I will be very careful to utilise protection,' he declared coolly. 'I will leave it to you to decide whether we will ever reach this magical day where we will sit down and *discuss* what comes *naturally* to half the world!'

Molly compressed her lips in silence. Djalia was not the most forward-thinking place. Having a wife was clearly fundamentally linked in Azrael's brain with having a family and he had taken it for granted that she would feel the same way. That she did not immediately wish to embrace motherhood was clearly unwelcome news to him.

'And now I must leave until we meet at the wedding tomorrow,' Azrael informed her and even his Mr Grumpy expression couldn't hide his relief at the prospect of escaping her unnatural attitude to conception. 'Your attendants will be arriving soon to prepare you as a bride.'

I'm falling in love with him, Molly registered in sudden dismay because she could see right through him just then and she could see that Azrael was both offended *and* deeply hurt. Her reluctance to conceive was being viewed as a rejection. It bothered her so much to see that in him that she was horribly tempted to put her arms round him to offer comfort. Unfortunately, that would be the wrong thing to do because Azrael had to learn that while it was apparently fine for him to make unilateral decisions for Djalia he could not expect the same freedom and authority within his marriage. *I want to keep you.* Spontaneous laughter bubbled up in her throat and she had to struggle to hold it back because he would definitely misinterpret that reaction.

She was tempted to tell him that she was not totally averse to the idea of becoming a mother but that would lead her down conversational roads she was not yet ready to travel with him. If she did choose to have a child, however, she wanted to plan the event, not find herself railroaded into it by an accidental conception. Furthermore, before she could even consider confidently embracing motherhood she needed to know that their marriage had a genuine future.

Unhappily, when she had agreed to stay married to Azrael on the basis that he would cover her grandfather's bills at the care home, they hadn't talked about so many things that they *should* have talked about. Although Molly always liked to know where she stood, she had never had that clarity with Azrael. They hadn't discussed sex, money, contraception, divorce or indeed any of the many complications waiting, it seemed, to trip them up and set them at odds. And now, evidently such discussions had strayed into such personal private territory that a frank exchange of views was liable to hurt or offend. What had happened to the man who had confided that he felt trapped and resentful once he'd learned that his false announcement that they were married had bound them in marriage by local law?

I want to keep you. What was she supposed

to say to that? What did she *want* to say to that? Molly thought it was far too soon to be making life-changing decisions and was more distrustful of the growing strength of her attachment to Azrael than ever. He was much more volatile than he seemed behind that cool, controlled façade of his, she acknowledged. Did he have feelings for her? Or did it all come down to amazing sex for him? Was he that basic? Or was she too suspicious and cynical?

CHAPTER NINE

'ZAHRA!' THE NEXT DAY, as afternoon faded into evening, Molly moved forward with a delighted smile to greet a surprisingly familiar face. The young Djalian woman had been her first pupil at the Djalian Embassy in London. The daughter of a senior diplomat, Zahra had so enjoyed Molly's lessons that before leaving London again she had recommended that Molly teach English to Tahir.

'Your husband believed that you would find my company useful,' the slender brunette told her shyly. 'I can act as an interpreter and also explain the bridal rituals.'

Molly's green eyes lit up with interest. 'I'm getting rituals?'

'The first royal bride to marry the King of Djalia this century? You're getting the full Djalian bridal treatment!' Zahra assured her with amusement. 'We're going out into the desert for it too. It would be a lot easier to do it all here but tradition means everything to our tribes.'

'You'll keep me right…thank goodness,' Molly whispered, hugely grateful for the support because without an interpreter she wouldn't be able to understand what was happening or why.

'It is a great honour for me and my family that I have been entrusted with such a role. My mother is very pleased and proud,' the Djalian brunette shared with a rueful laugh. 'Of course, my parents are probably hoping that you'll thrust me in the path of some eligible male but I have to tell you now…most of them are far too old for me. Too many of our young men died fighting Hashem and his troops.'

'That's sad,' Molly recognised.

'But the most important young man survived. Our King is revered for his bravery and his wisdom.'

'He is pretty special,' Molly muttered helplessly, reddening at Zahra's knowing smile as she made that statement.

'Yes. The King is the one person in Djalia who can unite all the different factions. He even keeps Prince Firuz on his side,' Zahra pointed out with a grimace. 'He's an old horror but we don't want to be at odds with our nearest neighbour and he did keep our current King safe from Hashem while he was still a boy.'

'Yes,' Molly conceded while thinking that Azrael had also paid a very high price for that protection with the punishments he had endured. A step ahead of her companion, she climbed into one of the air-conditioned rough-terrain vehicles parked in readiness outside the palace while the staff and luggage accompanying her piled into the two cars behind.

'But Prince Firuz won't even attend your wedding because Christian rites are being included. He is very rigid in his views,' Zahra admitted and then she winced. 'I'm being indiscreet. I should not be gossiping. My father would be ashamed of me—'

'Then Azrael would be equally ashamed of me,'

Molly countered wryly. 'I need to know what's going on and I don't want the sanitised version.'

The vehicle swept them only across the road to a flat plain where a helicopter awaited them. From the air, Molly peered out at the view of the palace from above and noted for the first time that there was a large, busy building site to the rear of it.

'New offices and kitchens,' Zahra informed her, but that was the entirety of their conversation during the flight because it was too noisy to chat.

They were set down in front of a large encampment of black tents and literally mobbed by a bunch of howling women the instant they appeared. Zahra explained to her that the howling was of a celebratory nature to welcome the bride. Her companion soon proved her worth by banishing the crowd, who wanted to see Molly bathe in the linen-lined copper bath she was confronted with.

'I'll stay at the entrance to make sure nobody comes in,' Zahra proffered, politely turning her back as Molly shed her clothing and climbed with great difficulty into the deep bath, which clouded the air with the aroma of scented oils. 'I have explained that in your culture bathing is always private.'

'I expect there's not much privacy in these tents between women,' Molly conceded, determined not to make a fuss about the differences and to fit in to the best of her ability, but very grateful not to be forced to put her naked body on show.

Having already bathed at the palace and washed her hair, Molly only made superficial use of the ceremonial bath and clambered out into a fleecy towel. Her wedding gown and lingerie awaited her in a connecting tent and she wasted no time in getting dressed, with Zahra well able and willing to hook up the back of her dress.

'It's a beautiful dress,' Zahra sighed, admiring the long lace sleeves and the slender silhouette of the elegant design Molly had chosen. 'Some brides here already wear Western gowns as one of their bridal changes. Photographs of you in this will encourage the fashion.'

A big silver box arrived to much fanfare.

'The bridegroom's gift to his bride,' Zahra explained.

'So, it's a tradition.' Less pleased by the awareness that Azrael was only doing what was expected of him rather than what he actually *wanted* to do, Molly opened the box and gazed down in awe at a fabulous set of emerald jewellery.

'These are royal jewels, passed from mother to son for the next generation. The King's mother, Princess Nahla, only wore them once when she married Prince Sharif.' Nimble fingers brushed Molly's nape as Zahra clasped the stunning necklace and passed her the glistening drop earrings.

Molly felt as though she were living history when she was escorted into yet another tent where Azrael awaited her, tall and grave in his traditional robes. His beautiful eyes were dark and serious below his lush screening lashes and she suspected that she was still unforgiven for her reaction to the possibility of a pregnancy. It really didn't matter, she admitted wryly to herself, because with one glimpse at Azrael the dulled ache between her thighs throbbed in wanton recollection, her entire body now shamefully attuned to his in the most mortifying way. The rising colour in her cheeks had nothing to do with the temperature.

The celebrant was an American minister and the service was short and sweet. Azrael's cool fingers slid a gold ring onto her wedding finger and, for the first time, Molly truly felt like a married woman.

In silence, Azrael admired the dress, which faithfully followed Molly's lush curves but which revealed barely any skin. He concentrated his attention on the rusty little marks scattered below her collar bone, trying to look on them as imperfections while recalling that the same freckles extended the stippling over her full creamy breasts. Unhappily for him he loved her freckles, and the urgent pulse at his groin infuriated him at so formal an occasion and when they had parted on such poor terms. How could he still hunger for a woman who did not want his child, who did not want to create a family with him? Who rejected a future of any kind with him? Who expected him to discuss what it was pointless to discuss? Her callous attitude, after all, had said all he needed to hear.

Molly had barely spent ten minutes in Azrael's presence before she was swept off again to be dressed appropriately for the signing of the marriage contract, which was the main event as far as her companions were concerned. Freed from the limitations of her Western wedding gown, Molly followed Zahra's advice and simply let the attendants dress her up as a traditional Djalian bride. Her hands and feet were ornamented with elaborate swirling henna patterns, her nails painted, her face made up with a much more dramatic application of cosmetics than she would personally have used. Finally, swamped in emerald-green brocade with a richly embroidered, buttoned blue under tunic sewn with pearls, she saw herself in a mirror and she didn't recognise her reflection because even her hair was hidden below an elaborate headdress. Throughout photos were taken by a female photographer. She wondered if Azrael would prefer her in such garb and whether it would bring a smile to his lean features.

She saw Azrael again in the presence of the solemn imam with the marriage contract laid out on a table and with Zahra and Butrus acting as witnesses. Coached by Zahra, she knew to allow the imam to ask her three times before she accepted and signed her name. She was settled down then into an elaborate wooden chair and then, to her dismay, hoisted high by a bunch of men and borne off into a big tent where a crowd awaited them. A drum was beating out a tattoo and women were wailing in apparent happiness. Molly pinned a fixed smile to her tense face as she was seated on a stage and watched Azrael brought in with loud drumming and even more pomp and ceremony. Kneeling at her feet, Zahra explained every stage, pointing out the tray of seven spices and the seven foods for purity arranged on a low table. She was brought a rose water and pomegranate cordial to drink and she was abstracted, marvelling at how stunning Azrael looked in his rich golden attire.

'I first saw his picture at the embassy in London,' she shared reflectively with Zahra. 'I didn't know who he was back then but I noticed him.'

'Women do tend to notice His Majesty.' Zahra smiled. 'Butrus mentioned that the first time the King saw you it was obvious that he was noticing you as well.'

Molly wondered if that was true, if it was possible that the same awareness that had initially electrified her had also affected Azrael. While musicians took their seats, dancers trooped in and tossed sweets to the guests. Azrael took a seat on the stage beside her as a table was arranged in front of them and Zahra excused herself.

'Zahra's been a wonderful help,' Molly confided. 'Explaining everything, translating for me. I didn't make any mistakes.'

'Everything at an occasion like this is new to you. Don't worry about making mistakes,' Azrael responded quietly.

A veritable feast of food was brought to them and Molly ate sparingly, too conscious of being the centre of attention to relax, but as the evening wore on and she watched Azrael take part in an astonishingly acrobatic traditional dance with actual swords her tension gradually ebbed because all around her people were happy and obviously having a good time. Every so often Zahra would approach her and bring people for her to meet, and the emeralds that still glowed round her neck were complimented many times and clearly a highly recognisable symbol of Djalian royalty that the guests liked to see on display.

They left the continuing festivities in the helicopter. 'Where are we going?' she asked Azrael.

'You'll see,' he parried. 'I hope I have made the right choice. Butrus thought I was crazy. The normal option would have been to remain in the encampment for the night.'

But Molly was grateful for any choice that took them away from the noisy partying and the almost suffocating attention of so many people. Privacy, she appreciated, was a gift Azrael rarely enjoyed and it would be the same for her because the local media would publish their wedding photos. At the same time, now that the cameras and

the audience were gone, how would they be together and how would Azrael behave?

Azrael lifted her out of the helicopter because
she was struggling in her capacious layers of brocade and silk and very much looking forward to
changing into something more comfortable and
shedding the heavy jewellery. In the darkness
she couldn't see where they were. All she could
see was an actual burning torch flaring against
a wall.

'Where are we?' she asked because she could
still see no artificial light and it was very quiet.
As she drew closer to the torch she saw that the
wall was a rock rather than an artificial creation
and her brow furrowed in confusion.

'It is a surprise. The helicopter will pick us up
again in the morning.' Azrael hesitated. 'I brought
you back to the cave for the night...'

A cave? *The* cave? Molly hinged her dropped
jaw shut again, grateful for the darkness. 'Wow,'
she said chirpily as if it were the best news she
had ever heard, because she was not stupid,
after all.

If Azrael was taking her back to the cave for their wedding night it was because he believed that was romantic and, since he was far too practical to be what she would have deemed a natural romantic, it signified a feat of imagination and effort on his part that she had to admire...even if she hated it.

'The stars are beautiful and the moon is full,' Azrael pointed out with pronounced determination as they trudged across the sand by the light of his cell phone.

My goodness, he's trying—he's trying so hard to make this special and you are an ungrateful cow, Molly scolded herself furiously. But to be fair, he had wrong-footed her because she *had* been planning to tell Azrael that she thought it would be wisest if they stopped having sex until they had both decided where their marriage was heading. Why? Because sex with Azrael killed her brain cells, she thought wildly, knowing there was no way she could drop the sex ban on him when he'd gone to the extreme lengths of taking her to a *cave* for the night. *I mean, how lucky am I to be the woman who gets to spend* another *night in the cave?*

A clutch of robed men moved away from the front of the cave, bowing to them both and addressing Azrael in their language. 'They are honoured to guard us tonight,' Azrael translated.

Molly contrived a brilliant smile and passed on into the cave…and found it transformed. There was a bed, a *proper* bed and lit lanterns everywhere. A seating area with rugs was arranged around a small fire as well as a table with covered dishes. Towels were heaped helpfully by the pool edge. Her contrived smile blossomed into a genuine smile and she spun back to Azrael to say spontaneously, 'You're not crazy. It was a wonderful idea.'

Smiling brilliantly, Azrael lifted her off her feet and set her down on the side of the bed.

'How on earth did you get a bed out here?' she whispered wonderingly.

'With the help of the same tribe who once brought supplies here for my mother and I,' he told her, watching as she tugged off her headdress and set it aside, shaking her head so her copper tresses spilled in bright spirals across her pale skin. She toed off her shoes and settled back against the heaped pillows, emerald earrings gleaming in the flickering candle light and acting as a reminder of something he had forgotten.

Azrael dug into his pocket to retrieve the ring box and handed it to her. 'I had it made to go with the necklace. I intended to give it to you before we signed the marriage contract but we were never left alone.'

'Better late than never,' Molly quipped, flipping open the box with inquisitive eyes, which widened at first sight of the huge oval emerald surrounded by diamonds. 'My word, this is gorgeous.'

Long brown fingers eased the ring out of its velvet bed and installed it on her wedding finger.

'Thank you,' Molly said warmly, understanding that the ring, given in private in contrast to the royal emeralds, was a personal gift.

No, she acknowledged, it very definitely wasn't the right moment for a serious discussion about whether or not their marriage had a future. He had made such an effort to please her that she was touched and surely a lasting future was more than implied by such an approach? *I want to keep you.* And she very much wanted to keep him, she conceded helplessly, watching him ditch his cloak and his head cloth and visibly shed the tension of the day.

'Would you mind if I took a dip in the pool?' Azrael enquired very politely. 'It's warm in here and it has been a long day.'

'Of course not,' she said, her body starting up a guilty hum at the very idea of him stripping. That very first glimpse of him in the same cave had turned her into a committed voyeur.

It was their wedding night but he was probably exhausted because he rarely enjoyed more than five hours of rest. Determined to get more comfortable, Molly stood up and began to remove the heavy emerald brocade robe.

'Allow me,' Azrael murmured, lifting it from her taut shoulders. 'Keep the emeralds on. It is a joy to see you wear them as I imagined.'

The hands she had been lifting to remove the weighty necklace dropped again and she settled back on the bed, striving not to look as though she was watching him undress when that was exactly what she was doing. He shed his tunic and stepped out of the loose linen pants he wore below, shedding his boxers at the same time, and the light fell on that long, elegant back she had so appreciated when she was half-unconscious and her breath betrayed her with a sudden indrawn hiss that made him whirl around, an ebony brow lifting in query.

'Your back...' she muttered hot-faced, sliding off the bed to approach him and step behind him, fingers lifting to trace the paler slashes of old scarring that marred his perfection. 'What happened to you?'

'Firuz had me whipped when I was seventeen,' he admitted tightly. 'Are the scars still so obvious?'

'No...no, they're very much faded,' she mumbled awkwardly, looking up at him with appalled eyes. 'Whipped? Literally *whipped*?'

Azrael jerked his chin in confirmation, clearly not a fan of pursuing the demeaning topic. Naked as a bronze god, he stalked over to the pool and stepped in, evidently expecting the dialogue to end there.

Molly hovered barefoot in the sand, wringing her hands. 'But...*why* would he do such a thing?' She tried but she could not hold the question in.

'When Firuz married my mother, he made an agreement with Hashem that neither my mother nor I would be allowed to become the focus of any rebel activity in Djalia against Hashem's rule. You must understand that my stepfather was afraid to anger Hashem because Quarein is a poor country with very little military capacity.'

'Yes...?' Molly breathed encouragingly.

But it didn't work. Azrael stretched out in the pool on the rocks in brooding silence, long black hair tousled around his big stiff shoulders. With a stifled sigh, Molly stripped off and, fighting her self-consciousness about her own body, she padded across the sand and stepped into the pool beside him, sinking down on the nearest flat rock.

'Yes?' she said again, refusing to surrender to that silence.

'From the moment Hashem executed my father, my mother became his most implacable enemy. She was a very brave woman. She raised funds for the rebels and was, until I became old enough, their *de facto* leader. She used Quarein as a safe house for both of us but, make no mistake, being married to Firuz was tough for my mother. He is a hard, judgemental man, who makes daily life difficult for those around him. When phone messages between his home and the rebels were intercepted by Hashem and brought to my stepfather's attention, it put my mother in grave danger.'

Molly grimaced. 'Of course it did.'

'To protect her I said that *I* had sent the messages and Firuz had me whipped. I believe he knew the truth and he let it go because in his own limited way he did care for my mother. As long as someone was punished Hashem was satisfied.'

'That's one of the secrets you thought I wouldn't want to know,' Molly guessed, smoothing a soothing hand down a bulging bicep. He was so modest, so reluctant to acknowledge his own courage for what it was. His sheer strength appealed to her on the most basic level because she knew that no matter what happened she could depend on Azrael. He was very strong and his innate need to protect those weaker than he was ran through him like a vein of solid gold.

'Why *would* you want to know such a thing?' Azrael demanded in honest bewilderment, twisting to study her with glittering dark golden eyes.

'I don't know, but I do,' Molly fielded dry-mouthed, somewhat belatedly noticing that, despite the icy temperature of the rock pool, he was fully aroused.

'Sometimes you are a very strange woman,' Azrael breathed thickly.

'But the differences between us are kind of fascinating,' Molly told him shakily, wanting so badly to touch him but afraid of doing it wrong.

Could she have but known it, there was no wrong in that line as far as Azrael was concerned. As he bent his head to claim her lush, inviting mouth, he carried her hand down his body, his breath tripping in his throat simply at the brush of her tiny fingers. Molly touched, stroked, in too awkward a position to really explore and he took care of that problem too by springing upright with a noisy splash and scooping her dripping body up to plaster it against his hot, wet body with an enthusiasm that suggested he was not as tired as she had assumed earlier.

'We'll get everything wet!' she gasped as he brought them both down on the bed.

And Azrael laughed with hearty amusement, spreading her out like a feast to be savoured, gazing down at her with wondering satisfaction. She didn't want his child, he reminded himself darkly before he sent that reality back into the burial ground at the back of his mind where he kept things that couldn't be changed. For the first time ever, he would live in the moment, savour its sweet pleasures and look neither forward nor back. On his wedding night, he was not the Djalian King, he was only a man, a man with a voracious appetite for the warmth and relaxation and pleasure that Molly represented.

Molly pushed him back against the pillows before he could kiss her again. 'My turn,' she told him with a hectically flushed face.

She knelt over him, wondering just where to start and spoilt for choice, her hands finding those wide brown shoulders and smoothing down over the hard buds of his male nipples to the corrugated lean muscle of his stomach and then lower, finding him, tracing him, rejoicing in the silky, tensile strength of him and the rise of his hips in response. With those stunning heavily lashed golden eyes welded to her every move she felt as though she had him at her mercy and she liked that feeling of power.

'I might be a little clumsy at this,' she warned him.

But Azrael was a willing sacrifice for any form of experimentation as he watched her lower her mouth to him. It was the most erotic thing he had ever seen. She licked, swiped and stroked and then she stretched her ripe lips around him and her head bobbed, copper ringlets trailing across his thighs like teasing ribbons. He had to fight to withstand the intensity of the pleasure, and when he couldn't tolerate it any longer he reached up and dragged her down to him to find her mouth again for his tongue, darting and exploring while his hands hungrily moulded the swollen bounty of her tightly beaded breasts and slid slower to trace the gloriously wet opening between her thighs.

'I want you now… I can't wait,' he groaned hoarsely, pushing her away and startling her as he sprang lithely off the bed to stalk over to the chest by the wall and rummage within it.

He tore open the packet and put on the condom while she watched with wide, equally impatient eyes for him to return to her. Her arms opened automatically for him, the throb between her thighs like a pulsing hum of eager welcome, a deep-seated ache that only he could satisfy. He drove into her hard and fast and she wanted to cry out but she was recalling those tribesmen outside the cave and the lack of doors and his controlled silence while she pleasured him. A tiny little whimper was wrenched from her and then there was nothing in her world but a nameless fear that for some reason he might stop, which she couldn't have borne.

Her heart thumped like an express train inside her body as Azrael reached a hard, insistent rhythm that made her buck and gasp with helpless excitement, her hips writhing, her entire skin surface burning up with the inexpressible wildness of the experience. The wicked delights of his possession went on and on and on until finally her body was thrust over the edge into climax. Delicious internal convulsions gripped her as the surge of pleasure washed over her in an unstoppable tide.

Still floating, she lay there cradled in Azrael's arms and feeling positively sunny in mood. It was slowly dawning on her that a baby with him, assuming she wanted to keep him, might even be a development she could welcome. Why? Because he was great in bed? Hardworking, honest, noble, gorgeous? Naturally there was also the beautiful ring and the cave setting, chosen for her benefit. But most of all her heart was his because he was a hero, who had suffered horrors she couldn't imagine, horrors he didn't even want to talk about for fear of upsetting *her*! Listening had almost broken her heart as she'd pictured Azrael, young and proud and vulnerable, accepting pain and humiliation to shield his mother. Now she was also picturing a little Azrael or a little girl and her heart began to go all floaty too.

'I was thinking…about a baby…' she murmured, stumbling over the words, having spoken before she even knew what she planned to say.

'We don't need to concern ourselves with that issue,' Azrael cut in, smooth and cutting as polished steel. 'Forget about that idea. I wasn't thinking rationally.'

Molly was disconcerted by that response; her lips framed a silent *oh* of perplexity and then hurt flared inside her where it didn't show because she felt rejected. He had thought the concept over just as she had done but he had reached a different conclusion. She had decided that it could be a very good idea to have a family with him but evidently, after further consideration, Azrael had decided against the same idea. He had changed his mind. He was entitled to do that. Did that mean that he no longer wanted to *keep* her? And if he had decided that, what was she supposed to be doing about it?

He hadn't asked her to fall in love with him, had he? It was her own fault that she had fallen head over heels in a process that had started the day she first saw that gorgeous portrait of him in the Djalian Embassy. But they had originally signed up for only a few months of being married and perhaps Azrael had realised that that option would still suit him best. Was there even a possibility that he was already planning that his next wife would be Princess Nasira? In fact, was Molly merely a kind of hiccup and an aberration in Azrael's planned marital journey?

That sneaking, humiliating suspicion kept Molly quiet when she would normally have spoken up and asked him why he had changed his mind. How could she *ever* be good enough or loveable enough for someone like Azrael? she questioned painfully. Compressing her lips, she shut out the mad tumult of her rushing thoughts and stamped on them hard when they tried to emerge and torment her again. Agonising over what could not be would not change anything. It would not change what Azrael felt and thought, but if she was sensible, and she so badly *wanted* to be sensible, she would begin trying to detach herself from unrealistic hopes and step back from her emotions.

CHAPTER TEN

'BUT THERE'S SOMETHING you're not thinking about,' Molly said as Azrael encouraged her to peruse the display of blueprints on the housing project. 'If you want to attract foreign experts to work on large developments that will run for years, you should consider setting up an international school—'

'An international school?' Azrael cut in with a frown. 'When our own education system is still so basic?'

'You have to prioritise,' Molly pointed out. 'You *need* the experts and they will be unwilling to sign up for long contracts without their families. They will want schooling for their children that will enable them to return to their home countries fully equipped to continue their education.'

Azrael's lean dark face took on a thoughtful aspect. Molly, he had learned, might tackle problems from a different angle but often came up with solutions that would not have occurred to him. She was clever and progressive. He studied her preoccupied face as she examined the blueprints he had recently had drawn up to house workers from abroad. She was correct. His country badly needed those professionals and their skills to drag Djalia into the twenty-first century, and to appeal to the right calibre of personnel they had to make the employment contracts attractive.

'Zahra is a teacher,' Azrael reminded her. 'Work with her to consider the setting up of an international school as soon as possible.'

Molly went pink with pleasure. 'Zahra will know far more than me.'

'But it was your idea. Run with it,' Azrael advised with a sudden charismatic grin. 'That is your punishment.'

Only it was anything but a punishment to be trusted with responsibility and to be with a man who invited and respected her opinions, Molly conceded inwardly. A mere two busy months into being Azrael's wife, Molly was failing dismally at the challenge of stepping back from her emotions and suppressing forlorn hopes. She loved Azrael and every moment she spent with him only made her love him more. When had anyone but Maurice ever listened to her with respect? When had any man ever wanted her to the extent that Azrael seemed to want her? But her childhood insecurity, her secret fear that she was not loveable or even truly wanted, still haunted her and filled her with the terror that she was living in a dream world and that sooner or later Azrael would take a good clear look at her and wonder what he was doing with her.

For that reason, every time she was tempted to ask Azrael how long he believed their marriage would last, fear strangled her voice and kept her silent. It was better to enjoy what she had while she still had it, she reasoned unhappily, rather than stress about how she would feel when it came to an inevitable end.

They had spent the first weeks of their marriage touring Djalia by helicopter and Molly had seen everything from the unspoilt desert that was still home to nomadic tribes to the oil fields and the greener, more mountainous region to the north of the country. Zahra had become her right-hand woman, acting as interpreter for both culture and language while also becoming a good friend. Molly, however, kept her secret fears to herself and simply tried not to dwell on them.

She had dived into her agreement with Azrael to stay married to him and he had dived in with an equal lack of forethought. In mysterious addition, since their official wedding the reality that their marriage was not supposed to be *real* seemed to have become a taboo subject. In the same way as Azrael had backtracked from the concept of her having a child with him he retreated at speed from any discussion of the future, with the result that Molly sometimes felt as though she were living in a soap-bubble fantasy.

That was why it was such a boost to her confidence to be asked to work on the building of an international school, because that would not be a short-term project. In the same way, she now asked herself, how could she truly feel that their marriage was only temporary when Azrael had taken the time and trouble to accompany her to London to meet her grandfather in his care home? Indisputably, Azrael treated Maurice like a family member. On their most recent visit, when Azrael had seen her happy tears because Maurice had enjoyed a little window of recognition and had connected again with Molly as his granddaughter for the first time in months, Azrael had been so supportive and compassionate in his understanding of how much that acknowledgement had meant to his wife.

In fact, Azrael was just about perfect in the husband stakes, Molly acknowledged helplessly. They had discovered that they both liked to keep fit and Azrael had a workout room on the ground floor where they exercised together early in the morning. Their values were also similar. On a spicier note, she was married to an urgent and exciting lover, who made her feel like the sexiest woman alive. He regularly gave her little unexpected gifts that ranged from perfume to jewellery to lingerie. Even the fact that he was quite embarrassed giving her the fancy lingerie that he loved to see her wear had made her love him still more.

Azrael, she was learning by degrees, was not that much more sophisticated than she was, because his life had not accorded him much opportunity for self-indulgence. The depth of his concern for his people, the endless hours he worked striving to get everything right, hugely impressed her. She didn't only love him, she also admired and respected him and she was incredibly happy being married to him.

But there were still little moments that could cruelly burst her cocoon of contentment. A couple of weeks after that first day of intimacy when Azrael had not used contraception with her, her period had arrived as usual. In truth she had been a tiny bit disappointed that she had not conceived and had scolded herself for that disappointment for it seemed wrong to want a child in a relationship that most probably would not last. There was also the sobering fact that Azrael had to think the same because he had been scrupulously careful to ensure that they did not run that risk again.

'At least you won't have that worry, then,' Azrael had commented, which had convinced her that he was thankful that she had not conceived.

What he had left unsaid in that nebulous remark had haunted Molly for weeks afterwards, reminding her, as evidently she had reminded him, that their marriage was temporary and at that some yet unnamed time in the future they would part and go for a divorce. And the prospect of losing Azrael choked Molly as much as a gradually tightening noose round her throat because she couldn't bear to contemplate the concept of suffering such a loss. In such a short space of time he had come to mean so much to her.

It had often seemed to Molly that throughout her life she had been unlucky and pretty much unloved. Only her grandfather had cared for her but, as her only refuge, what choice had he had? She had had nowhere else to go. Her father had let her leave without even asking her to visit because his wife's feelings had been more important to him than his daughter's. When she was younger she had often imagined confronting her dad about his lack of love and interest but had lost her nerve, knowing that being told her father couldn't care less about her would only hurt her more. And that was why she didn't have the courage to challenge Azrael and demand to know where their marriage was going, because she was afraid to force the issue. That pressure could easily push Azrael into bringing their relationship to a premature end, she thought fearfully.

Azrael's cell phone jangled and he dug it out. Within seconds she knew he was receiving word of some crisis because his whole demeanour changed. He vaulted upright, dark eyes flaring gold as expressions of alarm, concern and annoyance flashed across his darkly handsome features in rapid succession. He shot staccato questions, clenched his fingers into fists and strode about the room like a tiger confined in a too-small cage, coming up against walls and redirecting his steps with ferocious tension and impatience.

'I must leave,' he told her tightly when he had finished the call.

'What's happened?' she asked anxiously.

'You don't want to know.' Azrael muttered that dark assurance while his phone began to ring again.

'Of course I want to know,' she protested very quietly, reluctant to press harder when he was visibly under stress.

It was clear that the second call was of a different nature. Azrael closed his eyes and gritted his teeth and spoke in short, studied sentences in a much quieter tone to the second caller. Molly frowned, convinced she had heard Tahir's name, and she wondered how he was involved in whatever disaster had occurred. When Azrael had completed that call, he grimaced and by then Butrus was already knocking on the door, all flushed and troubled as if he had run up the stairs in a panic.

'It's a…er…diplomatic incident… I have to deal with this personally,' Azrael told Molly urgently and he strode off, talking in a low voice to Butrus.

'Oh, for goodness' sake!' Molly opined to the empty room in her frustration, wondering why Azrael had turned all secretive when it was more normal for him to be frank with her.

At Molly's request, Zahra joined her for lunch. It occurred to her that her companion was unusually constrained and she asked her why she was so quiet.

'I'm aware that you're dealing with a trying situation today,' the other woman remarked with an apologetic look on her pretty face.

Molly tensed. 'Situation?' she repeated.

'With Prince Tahir's arrival. I am sure the King does not wish to be dealing with such a problem either. On the one hand the Prince is his little brother seeking his support and on the other he is his wife's kidnapper, who frightened her a great deal,' Zahra extended uncomfortably. 'But it is a fact of life that a spoiled teenager who has been...er...disciplined and denied his usual freedoms will overreact—'

'I wasn't aware that you knew about the kidnapping,' Molly confided, wondering why Tahir had arrived in Djalia seeking his older brother's support.

'What the Prince did made such a big stink... I can call it that?' Zahra queried uncertainly as Molly nodded. 'Few with diplomatic connections remain ignorant of the true passage of events. Much has been learned from the exaggerated deference Prince Tahir received at the London Embassy in the King's name. Such a crime should *not* have been possible. Those who should have known better did not interfere to stop the Prince out of fear of causing offence and a bigger scandal. And I can never apologise sufficiently for being the woman who recommended that you teach the Prince.'

'Oh, for goodness' sake, that's not your fault!' Molly exclaimed. 'Tahir's sins are his own. I can understand that people were afraid to blow the whistle on him lest it rebound on them. But please tell me what Tahir has done now—'

'I will take care of that,' Azrael informed her drily from the doorway and Zahra shot upright and bowed very low, muttering apologies in her own language.

'Well, I shouldn't have had to ask Zahra,' Molly proclaimed defensively in receipt of a censorious appraisal from her husband. 'Why should I be the only person in the building who doesn't know what's going on?'

'Because I didn't want to upset you,' Azrael advanced bluntly as soon as they were alone again. 'Once again, Tahir has screwed up and I am involved in damage control. Although to be fair in this instance I would hold his father more to blame for his flight—'

Her brow furrowed. 'His...*flight*? He's run away from home?'

'Not only that.' Azrael's mouth took on a sardonic curve. 'He drove through a border checkpoint without stopping, hotly pursued by Quareini soldiers. There was a standoff between the forces on both sides of the border. The soldiers demanded the return of their quarry and the border guards refused because, when Tahir finally did stop, he was recognised and found to need medical attention. He has also claimed refugee status.'

Green eyes wide, Molly studied him in lively astonishment. 'Refugee status? *Tahir?*'

'He is legally within his rights…just,' Azrael said very drily. 'And I am torn between anger and sympathy while Prince Firuz is in an incandescent rage.'

'Tahir really does know how to dig himself into a deep hole.' Molly sighed, shaking her head.

'I am sorry my brother is here under this roof. That is distressing for you.'

Molly slid upright, her face troubled. 'No, it's not, Azrael. I am not that sensitive. It is more distressing for you to be plunged into this drama through no fault of your own.'

'You are generous,' Azrael breathed between gritted teeth. 'But as you say in the West I am caught between a rock and a hard place. He is my brother and I pity him because I *know* what he is going through right now…his father had him whipped in punishment for what he did to you.'

Molly turned white, horror flipping her stomach, because while she had wanted Tahir punished to discourage him from any similar behaviour in the future she felt sick at the thought of that much physical violence being employed as a deterrent.

'Firuz always goes way over the top,' Azrael declared heavily. 'Tahir was cosseted and spoiled from birth because he is an only child, but you cannot raise a future leader with such selfish indulgence and then expect him to take brutal punishment like an adult. Tahir is distressed and overwhelmed by what he has brought on himself. After he has cried in my arms like a frightened child, how can I force him to return to Quarein with his father?'

Molly was pacing and thinking fast. 'Let him stay until the dust settles and tempers have cooled. There's nothing to be gained from allowing an immediate confrontation between father and son. I would concentrate on keeping a lid on the whole business.'

A slow appreciative smile formed on Azrael's wide sensual mouth while he watched her lovely pensive face. 'What do you think I have been doing? Molly, you are a wife in a thousand not to demand that I throw Tahir out.'

'By the sounds of it, he's paid for what he did to me...'

And if he hadn't kidnapped me, I'd never have met you, she was thinking, but she bit back that revealing statement, her cheeks warming to a hot pink and a deep, visceral sexual awareness darting through her slender body as she collided with Azrael's striking dark golden gaze.

Stray recollections of the night before teased at her memory and the heat in her cheeks arrowed down into her pelvis, encouraging a wanton warm slickness at her feminine core. She shifted position and folded her arms with a jerk, ashamed that Azrael could make her so weak and needy at the most unsuitable moments. Her breath caught in her dry throat.

'I will still make arrangements to have him moved elsewhere once the doctor gives us permission,' Azrael declared with determination, stalking over to the window to detach himself from the carnal thoughts that afflicted him whenever he was in his wife's presence. It was a lust, a primal need and hunger that never dimmed no matter how often he enjoyed the glories of her lush body. Having Molly in his bed had only spawned a powerfully addictive craving.

'Is he that bad?' Molly questioned in consternation.

Bold profile silhouetted against the light, Azrael jerked his strong chin in grim confirmation. 'Firuz has acted like an idiot and his own worst enemy. He has lost his son's love and trust and it will take a long time to rebuild their relationship.'

'He did the same to you.'

'But I was not of his blood and I was a good deal tougher than Tahir has ever had to be. Unfortunately, what Tahir did to you seriously frightened his father. Firuz has a great fear of scandal and sexual licence and he could not countenance that misbehaviour in anyone, least of all his own son. Now what is done is done and there is no easy solution.'

Molly wandered over to him and rested her hands on his rigid shoulders. 'None of this is your fault. You're stuck in the middle but don't get worked up about it. Tahir did wrong and now his father has done wrong. Keep that in mind.'

Azrael swung back to her. 'I hate that this is happening, because I didn't want you to be reminded of your ordeal,' he admitted grimly.

'Sometimes I think you just love an excuse to beat yourself up and take the worries of the world on your shoulders,' Molly censored him gently. 'You didn't ask for this and you can't magically solve it. Tahir and his father must sort it out. Will the newspapers write about this?'

'No. Thankfully our press are restrained. There will be rumours but nobody will see any benefit in embarrassing our closest neighbour or in embarrassing me because Tahir is my brother,' he completed wryly. 'He is so irresponsible, so explosive in his defiance of his father—'

'Stop thinking about it,' Molly urged.

'We have to go out this evening. There is a reception at the Quareini Embassy to which we have been invited. Firuz is presiding over it. It will be a gloomy occasion in the mood he will be in. Even before he arrives he is demanding that his son be returned to him.'

'We'll manage,' Molly responded quietly.

His lean brown hands came up to frame her face and tilt up her mouth for the descent of his marauding mouth. The kiss smouldered hotter than fire and she melted down deep inside and shifted closer, leaning into the hard, muscular strength of his big body. He lowered his hands to curve them round her waist until an urgent knock sounded on the door and his head lifted and he loosed a low groan of frustration.

Accustomed to such interruptions, Molly retreated several steps, her cheeks flushed, her mouth swollen from the erotic demand of his. Azrael called out an invitation and Molly headed off to dress for the embassy reception, deciding that if she was finally going to meet Tahir's father, the difficult Prince Firuz, she would opt to wear something traditional, rather than fashionable.

'Should I wear the emeralds tonight?' she asked Azrael when he strode past her, stark naked, to step into the shower she had had completed by telling Butrus to get hold of a plumber who knew how to install a shower, which the castle plumber evidently did not. She savoured her view of her husband's lithe bronzed beauty. 'I don't want to remind your stepfather of your late mother.'

'She never wore them again after my father's death,' he dismissed. 'Wear them.'

Azrael frowned a little when he saw her garbed in the long embroidered Djalian dress. 'Why are you wearing that?'

'Your stepfather isn't very westernised, is he?'

'My wife should ignore such prejudices. Wear your own clothes,' Azrael advised.

A little flushed by the effort of changing again at the very last minute, Molly donned her form-fitting green dress and high heels and Azrael clasped the emerald necklace for her. 'You look gorgeous,' he murmured huskily, poised behind her so that she could drink in his reflection in the mirror. 'I plan to ravish you later but only *after* you take that devil's garment off.'

Recalling his struggle with the super-stretchy

dress, Molly giggled, feeling wonderfully carefree after the challenging events of the day. But before they could head down the stairs to leave, Azrael was intercepted by Butrus, who announced that the doctor wished to consult him about Tahir's condition.

Ten minutes later, having been assured that Azrael would join her as soon as he was able, Molly walked alone into the reception being staged in a drab, scantily furnished room. A small, spare man with a tight little mouth, forbidding dark eyes and a greying goatee beard headed straight for her accompanied by the ambassador, who performed an introduction. Even as she explained that Azrael had been delayed, Molly was very tense. The coldness in the Prince's gaze was no surprise to her because she knew that she had to be the very last woman he would have wanted Azrael to marry. Even worse, she was the young woman whom Tahir, his son, had kidnapped.

'Your Highness,' she said smoothly, having been coached well by Zahra.

Polite conversation was exchanged but the

strain in the atmosphere was unmistakeable. Molly assumed that everyone present was aware of Tahir's unsanctioned flight from Quarein and his father's guardianship as well as his current residence within his brother's household. The ambassador was hailed by a guest and moved to the other side of the room.

'You are, I must assume, a very clever woman,' Prince Firuz remarked stiffly.

Molly's slim shoulders straightened as she decided to take the comment at face value and not look for double meanings. 'Why do you think that?' she parried quietly.

'First you tempt my son to the edge of madness and then you seduce and marry my stepson,' the older man murmured in an embittered undertone. 'But I assure you that you will never be Queen here.'

'Is that so?' Molly queried without any expression at all, determined not to be drawn into defending herself. He was an unpleasant man and she had been well warned of the fact but that didn't mean that she had to stoop to the same level.

'My niece, Nasira, will be Queen of Djalia when Azrael takes her as his second wife. She will be his *true* wife,' he proclaimed with a pity-ing smile. 'You are only a distraction, an amuse-ment, and if you are not prepared to share your husband with another wife I would advise you to bow out now.'

Molly could feel perspiration beading her brow but she refused to react. Her legs felt as weak as cooked spaghetti under her, her knees trembling with the rigidity of her stance. She felt sick, lit-erally felt the blood ebb from below her skin. A second wife? She refused to even consider that possibility but knew that it was yet another sub-ject that she and Azrael had not discussed and she had no idea of his views. She knew his grand-father, the infamous Hashem, had had multiple wives. One extra wife might even seem quite modest in comparison, she found herself reflect-ing insanely.

An arm settled against her stiff spine and Azrael's voice sounded above her head as he engaged the older man in conversation in their own language. She guessed that he was bringing the Prince up to date on Tahir's condition and there was a freezing silence at one point before Firuz simply glowered and turned on his heel without another word to stalk out of the room.

'We'll circulate for half an hour and then we'll leave,' Azrael breathed tautly. 'You should've brought Zahra with you—'

'We were already running late and she had gone home for the evening. It seemed pointless to disturb her when you were still expecting to come,' she fielded, proud that her voice was level.

But it seemed that Azrael was much too acute an observer to be fooled. 'You're very pale. What did he say to you?'

'I'll tell you later...*not* here,' she muttered uncomfortably, not even sure she wanted to share what had been said to her.

It was nonsense and nasty nonsense at that, she told herself squarely. How could she even credit such a suggestion? Prince Firuz was furious that

Azrael had married an ordinary Englishwoman instead of his multi-talented and regal niece. He also blamed Molly for her abduction by his son. And going by the way he had treated his stepson, he didn't much like Azrael either.

'Tahir is receiving treatment but he is in no state to travel even if he wanted to, which he does not,' Azrael divulged when they finally left the reception and had the privacy to talk in their car. 'I cannot turn my back on him. He has no one else but I also have a duty to you as my wife—'

'Don't fuss,' Molly urged wryly. 'I can cope if I must with a very large, disgruntled teenager, particularly if he's unhappy. Whatever else he is, he's your brother and he came to you for help. And no, *don't* tell me that I'm being generous or forgiving because forgiveness doesn't come into it at this stage. I'm being practical. We can't throw him out and even Tahir deserves a second chance.'

'Nasira urged me to throw him out to force him to return to Quarein,' Azrael proffered, startling her.

Molly turned her head, green eyes sparkling

with annoyance. 'I wasn't aware you were in contact with her.'

'We spoke when you returned to London to prepare for our wedding and since then she has stayed in touch by text.'

'How did you speak to her when I was in London?' Molly questioned sickly.

'I attended a charity dinner in Dubai while you were away. I was surprised when Firuz arrived with Nasira. I could see that she was uncomfortable socialising in mixed company without her veil. I felt sorry for her,' Azrael startled her even more by confessing. 'It was obvious to me that her uncle had put pressure on her to make that public appearance so that she could meet me again.'

Molly swallowed hard and the silence dragged. He had seen Nasira recently and he was *texting* the other woman. She felt sick and shaky again, as if the foundations of her world were crumbling beneath her. *Texting!* she thought again. She hadn't expected to hear that. Relations with Nasira were clearly much more friendly than she could ever have guessed. Did Azrael win points for being honest about that fact? Bad deeds could hide in plain sight, she reminded herself unhappily.

'You said you'd tell me what Firuz said to you—'

'Not right now. I've got a bit of a headache,' Molly framed jerkily.

Azrael was frowning. 'He upset you—'

'Now you're imagining things,' Molly complained, grateful as their transport pulled in at the castle entrance. She needed to compose herself before she confronted him, she reflected dizzily. Texting? *Sexting?* How could she possibly know? There was much more of a relationship between Nasira and Azrael than she had naïvely realised and that shook her because in the light of that information Firuz's allegations no longer seemed quite so far-fetched.

On automatic pilot, Molly climbed out of the car and sped through the hall straight for the stairs. Azrael strode after her, anger beginning to stir in his dark eyes because Molly was usually open with him and he was exasperated by her sudden evasiveness.

'I insist on knowing exactly what Firuz said to you before I arrived.'

Pale and rigid with self-control, Molly turned from the bedroom window. 'You *insist*?'

'I do.' Azrael didn't back down an inch from that arrogant demand. 'You are clearly upset—'

Anger stirred in Molly. He had been texting Nasira. He had deliberately misled her about his relationship with the other woman, letting her assume it was of no account. 'I'm upset because I can't trust you,' she told him starkly. 'You've been texting another woman—'

Azrael rolled his eyes at her and her temper rocketed even higher. 'Not in the sense that you mean. Nasira would be very shocked to think you suspected her of anything of that nature—'

'Oh, would she, indeed?' Molly spat, unimpressed. 'Yet she's been texting a married man! Firuz wanted you to marry Nasira before I came along, didn't he?'

'I will admit that he suggested her but at the time I wasn't seriously considering marrying anyone. I'm still young and I'm currently very busy.

If I had a plan, it was to put off marriage for a few years,' he admitted with a wry slant of his expressive mouth. 'A good marriage requires time and attention. Waiting to make that commitment made better sense.'

Appraising the cool set of his lean, darkly handsome features, Molly turned away to hide her emotions because every word he had said only reminded her that he had not wanted a wife in the first place and had only asked her to stay for a while for the sake of appearances. It was as though a cruel cold wind blew away all her warm, happy memories of the past two months.

Unhappily, staying on in Djalia, taking part in that wedding and all that had followed had blurred every boundary that she had originally assumed they would try to respect. But Azrael hadn't tried to do that; he hadn't recognised limits; he hadn't behaved like a man who was 'faking it'; he had behaved like a newly married man with a bride he desired and cherished. And now it all felt too good to be true, as if someone like her could not possibly deserve such a happy ending. All the insecurities that Molly had held at bay had been unleashed by Firuz's intervention.

'So, Nasira,' she began afresh.

'Nasira is blameless, guilty only of being firmly beneath her uncle's thumb,' Azrael incised impatiently.

Hurt by his immediate defence of the other woman, Molly stiffened until she felt as if she had a steel rod laced into her spine. 'Blameless?' she questioned thinly.

'I assure you that there has been no flirtation, no sexting or whatever you call it!' Azrael snapped back at her in exasperation. 'She was merely advising me not to get involved in the trouble between Firuz and his son and in a normal situation it would be good advice, but this is *not* a normal situation. She is not aware that my brother is threatening to kill himself if I send him back to his father!'

Molly's concern about Nasira and her texting had to take a back seat at that instant and she stared back at him in consternation. 'He's suicidal?'

'The psychiatrist we called in believes that a few quiet weeks away from his home environment will give Tahir the chance to regain his stability.'

'I'm sorry… I had no idea that he needed that kind of medical attention,' Molly muttered uncomfortably, looping her hair off her warm brow because she felt deeply uncomfortable. 'You should've explained that.'

'I was planning to tell you but I myself only understood Tahir's state of mind this evening after the psychiatrist spoke with me. Given time and peace he will improve.' Azrael heaved a sigh. 'In law, my brother is still a minor, however, and I hope Firuz will see the wisdom of leaving him here with me until he is, at least, on the road to recovery. Firuz could go through the courts and demand his return but I doubt that he would risk the adverse publicity that that would invite.'

'I didn't realise,' Molly said again. 'I should've guessed when you said he was behaving like a child.'

'He'll mend,' Azrael declared in a curt tone

of finality. 'Now let us return to your obsession with Nasira and the occasional texts we have exchanged. There is nothing for you to be concerned about.'

'I am *not* obsessed!' Molly broke in heatedly. 'But you should've been more frank about your relationship with her, particularly when Firuz went out of his way to ensure that you met her before our wedding. Perhaps he was hoping that you'd ditch me at the last minute!'

Cool as ice, Azrael frowned and sent her a questioning glance. 'Molly, think about what you're saying,' he urged in a tone that suggested she was being unreasonable. 'Think of the family relationship involved. I knew Nasira as a child because she was my stepfather's niece. Why would I behave in such a way? Think the facts through. We were already legally married before our public wedding, so there was no possibility of any ditching.'

Mortification and anguish slivered through Molly because what he was saying wasn't enough to disprove his former stepfather's insinuations.

She lifted her head high, faint tremors assailing her rigid figure. 'But Firuz may have hoped that, having met her again, you might be prepared to consider taking a second wife.'

Azrael shot her an arrested appraisal, dark golden eyes bright as flames. '*While* I was still married to you?' he demanded with incredulity.

Molly lifted her chin in challenge. 'Well, it's a possibility, isn't it?'

'No, it is not. I will not follow in Hashem's footsteps and take more than one wife. That practice is frowned on in Djalia, although I admit that it is still common in rich families in Quarein. My mother agreed to marry Firuz only after he promised that she would be his sole wife,' Azrael told her grimly.

Molly smoothed her dress down over her hips with damp trembling hands. 'I've offended you, haven't I?'

Azrael compressed his lips, battling back the kind of anger that would do him no favours in a delicate situation. But was that how he impressed her? As the kind of man who would take a wife and then seek another? It dawned on him that the waiting game he had chosen to play in his marriage had created all too many grey areas between them. He had said nothing, he had tried to *show* rather than tell, but it looked as if he hadn't done too well in that department.

At that point, Molly told him word for word what Prince Firuz had said to her, from the insinuation about her having tempted Tahir to the allegation that Azrael still planned to wed Princess Nasira. 'And then I find out she's already texting you!' she completed. 'How is that supposed to make me feel?'

Unbowed, Azrael stood his ground. 'Nasira is only a pawn in Prince Firuz's ambition to gain greater influence in Djalia and now he's trying to use her to cause trouble between us. He lied to you because he knows me well enough to know that I would not take an additional wife under any circumstances. For that reason it would suit him very well if our marriage broke down,' he pointed out smoothly.

'Under *any* circumstances?' Molly pressed, her fingernails biting into her palms with tension.

'Not under any circumstances,' Azrael confirmed, black-lashed dark golden eyes welded to her pale, anxious face. 'I am shocked that you could listen to Firuz and credit his lies for so much as a moment.'

A tad of the tension in her slight shoulders lifted and she snatched in a sudden ragged breath to re-fill her straining lungs. 'OK,' she conceded very quietly.

'Why would you think such a thing of me? A *second* wife? Are you not wife enough for me?' Azrael demanded.

Molly reddened and shifted her feet. 'We don't have a real marriage—'

'It feels real enough to me. It has from the out-set.'

Molly jerked a shoulder in an uneasy movement. 'But we made an agreement that the marriage would only last for a few months.'

'And then I said that I wanted to keep you and I meant every word of it. I am not the sort of man

who says such words lightly. It was not a joke,'
Azrael breathed with simmering impatience, as
if he could not understand her lack of faith in
him. 'Did you think I was joking? Shooting you
a smart line? Teasing in some way?'

Feeling cornered, Molly bridled. 'I knew you
weren't joking when you said it but you never said
anything more—'

'What more *was* there to say?' Azrael raked
back at her in driven frustration. 'I spoke plainly.
I made it clear that I did not wish our marriage
to be temporary. I told you that I wanted you for
ever—'

'No, you did not!' Molly flung back at him with
vigour. 'You didn't say that. You said you wanted
to keep me and that was that.'

'That's unfair. How was I to open my heart
when you were giving me no encouragement to
believe that you felt the same way?' Azrael demanded rawly. 'And then when you declared that
you did not want to have my child it was obvious
that you did not feel what I felt.'

'And what *do* you feel?' she dared to press,

leaving aside his conviction that she didn't want his child.

'You should *know* what I feel for you,' Azrael countered angrily. 'I have been obvious in my feelings. I may not have used the words but I have tried to prove my love in every way I could…'

Molly felt a shade dizzy and she backed to the side of the bed, using her hands to stabilise herself against the side of the mattress. 'Prove your love,' she echoed weakly. 'You're saying that you love me?'

'I think I fell in love with you in the cave but I didn't recognise it as love until after the wedding. When I thought you'd lied to me about your grandfather I was devastated. That's why I lost my temper,' he explained tautly. 'I have never felt such a connection with a woman. I have never been privileged to share such passion before. Of course, I wanted to keep you. Of course, I want you to be my wife for ever. I know I will never feel for any woman what I feel for you.'

'You know, when you finally start talking, you are definitely worth listening to,' Molly framed shakily, tears stinging the backs of her eyes because she was overwhelmed by what he was telling her. 'But you don't always listen carefully to what I say. I did *not* say I did not want your child. I only said it was something that should be planned, something that should only happen ideally in a secure relationship, and I didn't know we had that.'

'We are in a secure relationship if you want to stay married to me.'

Molly flung herself at him. 'Of course I want to. I love you too.'

Hands linking round her waist to hold her close, Azrael smiled, brilliantly, blindingly, dark golden eyes stunning. 'Well, you didn't say the words either so how can you hold my silence against me?'

'And why didn't I guess that you loved me when you set up our wedding night in the cave?' Molly mumbled guiltily, both arms tightly wrapped round him, little tremors of relief passing through her slender frame. 'I was stupid. I was trying to keep my feelings under control, only that never worked around you.'

'We are both very passionate people,' Azrael pointed out with appreciation, gazing down into her upturned face with a warmth and adoration she marvelled that she had not recognised until that moment. 'And with you I feel that I can be myself. I don't have to put on a show. I don't have to pretend. I can relax and you don't expect me to be perfect—'

'Right now you're at your highest ever approval rating.' Molly sidled back a step to haul her stretchy dress up and over her head and let it fall, revelling in the gleam of his admiring gaze over her matching silky underpinnings.

Engaged in shedding his clothing at speed, Azrael grinned at her, scooping her up in his powerful arms to settle her down on the bed. 'I can work with that,' he teased, a vision of lithe bronzed muscular perfection as he came down to her emanating predatory sexual power.

'I'd like a few more months before we think of starting a family,' Molly told him honestly. 'I love the idea but I don't think I'm quite ready to take the plunge yet.'

Azrael laughed. 'I too would like to have you all to myself for a little longer…but your rejection stung that day. For me then, having a child was the obvious next step—'

'Only not before you told me you loved me and wanted me to be your wife for ever,' Molly qualified.

'You should've realised that if I was willing for you to have my child I had no intention of ever letting you go,' he traded softly. 'We both want the security that neither of us enjoyed as children for our own family.'

'Yes.' Touched that he understood that, Molly stretched up and brushed her lips across his wide sensual mouth, knowing that he would understand that invitation even better. Happiness was bubbling through her in a wash of giddy energy. Azrael was hers, absolutely body and soul hers, and she couldn't stop smiling at that revitalising knowledge, that wonderful promise for her future.

'And every year on our anniversary we'll make

a trip back to the cave,' Azrael declared with romantic fervour. 'That is where we began.'

'You never did tell me what happened to the bra which went missing,' Molly reminded him playfully.

Azrael winced. 'I tore it when it caught on the towel. It was ruined, so I buried it—'

'You *buried* it?' Molly burst out laughing, tickled by his embarrassment.

'That wasn't an explanation I wanted to make at that point in our relationship.' Azrael smiled down at her while he ran a seemingly lazy hand down a pale thigh and she shivered, all hot and needy in secret places.

And the silence fell, broken only by little whispers and moans and all the sounds of a happy couple fully engaged in sharing the love that blessed them. Molly told him how much she loved him. Azrael told her he loved her more. She argued, he pointed out how patiently he had tried to prove how much he cared for her without speaking the words. She told him he should have spoken up sooner. He told her she talked too much and he kissed her, and halfway through the kiss she surrendered and let him win an argument for a change.

Almost three years later, Molly strolled into the castle's main ground-floor reception room, which had been reclaimed from office use once the new offices and conference rooms in the rear extension had opened. Since the birth of their son, Sharif, two years earlier, the royal family of Djalia had required more space. Her brother-in-law, Tahir, was hunkered down playing with toy cars and his nephew.

A regular visitor to his brother's home, Tahir was on leave from his officer training course at Sandhurst in the UK. Prince Firuz had suffered a heart attack and his health was failing, and recently Tahir had had to take on more and more of his father's official duties in Quarein. Working through his troubled teen years had changed the younger man a great deal. He had come back from his nervous breakdown stronger and more mature and had gone straight to military school for two years, weathering the tough regime with Azrael's support.

'Molly,' he greeted her warmly. 'Your son is very demanding. Every time I try to leave he cries and clutches at my legs.'

Molly scooped up the boisterous toddler, who had his mother's green eyes and his father's black hair. She had conceived almost as soon as she'd tried and, although she had had to have a C-section because Sharif was a large baby, she had had an easy pregnancy and she was thinking of trying for a second child the following year. There were so many other claims on her time, she acknowledged thoughtfully. She sat on the board of governors for the international school and, now that the pace of modern change in Djalia had become unstoppable, she was very busy.

When she needed clothes now she could shop in Jovan, and when she walked through the shopping mall and saw other young women wearing Western fashion she felt proud that she had helped Azrael bring about that transformation. Business and investment were booming in Djalia and the tourist trade had taken off like a rocket, encouraged by Molly's enthusiastic PR campaign on behalf of her adopted country. But her proudest and happiest moments were still those she spent with her husband and son.

'Sometimes, Sharif's a manipulative little monster,' she said fondly of her astute two-year-old. 'Azrael and I are the only two people in the building who ever say no to him.'

'Keep on saying it,' Tahir advised wryly. 'If I had heard that word more often when I was a kid I would never have gone off the rails.'

'But you're a different person now,' Molly pointed out as he vaulted upright, looking very serious. 'I wish you could stay for longer.'

Tahir grimaced. 'Duty calls and I don't mind it as much now that I can see how much my father needs me at home.'

'Has he mellowed any?' Molly enquired ruefully.

'No, my father doesn't do mellow,' Tahir declared with amusement. 'But we're getting along better in spite of our differences.'

Azrael strode in, tall, dark and devastatingly handsome. A simple glimpse of Azrael still gave Molly's susceptible heart a revitalising jolt. Her delight in him never seemed to ebb and she revelled in their closeness. Over three years into their marriage she could not have been happier. It was almost a year since her grandfather had passed away. Molly had spent most of Maurice's last weeks with him in the UK and she had been heartbroken when she had finally had to say goodbye to the old man that she loved. Azrael had been an irreplaceable source of strength and comfort during that difficult period.

Sharif raced across the floor to throw himself at his father with a whoop of excitement. Some rough play took place and Azrael tickled him, grinning as the toddler succumbed to helpless giggles.

'I wish I'd had that much fun growing up,' Tahir muttered ruefully.

'You can give your own children that fun,' Molly told him gently.

Tahir rolled his eyes in mock horror. 'That's

years away!' he exclaimed, giving her a casual hug. 'Look after yourself.'

'And you,' she said warmly, as ever amazed at the depth of affection she had developed for her husband's once troubled kid brother. It had grown during the weeks he'd spent living with them and recovering from his breakdown. She had gradually come to see that Tahir had abducted her more out of a desire for her warmth and approval than from more romantic motives. Still grieving for his mother and unhappy in his home life, Tahir had made a desperate grab for what he'd mistaken for love and as the two of them had come to understand that reality their mutual discomfiture had faded to be replaced by family affection.

'He's turning out OK,' Azrael pronounced with quiet pride after Tahir had departed. 'I can see the man he will become now. Strong, steady, sensible. He doesn't have his father's brutal repressive streak or my hot temper.'

'Yes.' Molly rubbed her cheek lovingly against a broad shoulder, drinking in the familiar scent of him. 'You're volatile enough for both of you.'

'I control it,' he reminded her.

Molly grinned against his shoulder because he didn't control that marvellously explosive, passionate streak in their bed and she was addicted to the excitement he gave her. Sharif went off with his nanny to have his tea, leaving Molly and Azrael alone.

'I have a little surprise for you,' Azrael told her, hustling her upstairs to their bedroom.

Azrael was a great fan of giving her surprises but he didn't always get it right. Their first Christmas together he had bought her a piano, only to wince in surprise when he'd listened and realised that she had not played in years. Music lessons had followed and now she practised daily and could turn out a creditable performance on the keys. These days she usually only saw his Mr Grumpy expression when he was forced to travel and leave her behind. He hated being separated from his family.

'It took a long time to track these down and considerable persuasion to get the new owners to part with them,' Azrael told her, handing her two small boxes. 'But I was determined that you would be reunited with your family heritage.'

'Azrael,' Molly sighed, wondering what on earth he was talking about. 'A family as ordinary as mine—unlike yours—doesn't have what you would call a heritage...'

'A man with Hashem in his family tree has no false pride and few illusions about his supposedly illustrious bloodline,' Azrael contradicted.

Molly opened the boxes and her lashes fluttered up on amazed eyes. 'My grandmother's brooch and ring!' she gasped, staring down at the glittering diamonds in disbelief. 'How on earth—?'

'They are very fine stones and very old. We will probably never know how they came into your *ordinary* family, but perhaps they were passed down from a wealthier generation to yours,' he suggested, smiling as she put the ring on her finger with tears of joy shining in her lovely green eyes.

'This means so much to me!' Molly admitted

chokily. 'I am *so* moved that you would go to that much trouble to get these back for me.'

'I was touched that you would make such a sacrifice to care for Maurice and I was determined that they should be recovered for you,' Azrael murmured, brushing a sparkling tear from her cheek with a gentle fingertip. 'You're so loyal and loving…and I am so very fortunate to have found you. I adore you, Molly mine.'

'And I adore you.'

In reward, Azrael brought his firm, sensual mouth down on hers, tasting her with powerful pleasure while hunger sizzled through Molly's shapely body like a living flame.

'I was planning to save them until we visited the cave to celebrate our anniversary next week,' Azrael confided as he came up for air again. 'But once I received them, I *had* to give them to you. I couldn't wait to see your beautiful face light up.'

'Mr Gorgeous, you are my every dream come true,' Molly told him joyfully.

'I can live with that label even less easily than I

can live with Glorious Leader,' her plain-speaking husband told her firmly.

'But I can't live without you,' Molly declared sunnily, lost in those stunning dark golden eyes locked to her smiling face.

* * * * *

β